THE HAUNTING
OF GREY HILLS
Forests of the Night

JENNIFER SKOGEN

E

EPIC
Press

Forests of the Night
The Haunting of Grey Hills: Book #2

Written by Jennifer Skogen

Published by EPIC Press™
PO Box 398166
Minneapolis, MN 55439

Cover design by Dorothy Toth
Images for cover art obtained from iStockPhoto.com
Edited by Melanie Austin

Library of Congress Cataloging-in-Publication Data

Skogen, Jennifer.
Forests of the night / Jennifer Skogen.
p. cm. — (The haunting of Grey Hills ; #2)
Summary: The Door of the Dead is open, and Macy hones her
newfound powers destroying the ghosts who emerge. When she meets a ghost
who reminds her of her dead brother, Macy's dangerous friendship grows
stronger leaving everyone to decide, what secrets are worth keeping,
and what price are they willing to pay for them.
ISBN 978-1-68076-030-9 (hardcover)
1. Ghosts—Fiction. 2. High schools—Fiction. 3. Supernatural—Fiction.
4. Haunted places—Fiction. 5. Young adult fiction. I. Title.
[Fic]—dc23
2015932719

EPICPRESS.COM

To Brian, for all of the forests we've walked together, and the many miles ahead

Chapter One

Macy wore black gloves to Nick's funeral. They itched. She picked at one of the cuffs while she sat in the front pew, waiting for the last few people to leave. It was stuffy in the small church, and someone had opened a window. Outside the rain fell—a constant hush through the trees.

The wooden pew was hard, and her left leg started to go numb. Macy uncrossed her legs and stretched them out in front of her, rolling her ankles first to the right, then to the left. Her black tights made her shins look shiny, and her dress was too short, but it was the only black one she had with pockets.

A little girl sat playing jacks at the front of the church, just a few feet from Macy. During the entire service she had bounced the ball on the hardwood floor and then scooped up four or five silver jacks at a time. Over and over again. The girl had short blond hair tied up in bows, and snowman-patterned pajamas. Every now and then she would look up at Macy and yawn, blinking her eyes slowly, like a kitten. Whenever she yawned, Macy had to yawn too. She hoped no one saw her yawning at her own brother's funeral.

Macy wondered if the little girl knew she was dead. She hoped not. That was probably the worst—to actually know that you're a ghost and that your body is somewhere rotting in the ground. Macy used to think that she wanted to be cremated, like her brother, but after watching all those people in the gym burn she couldn't stand the thought of someone setting her body on fire. Even if she were already dead. Especially then— when there was nothing she could do about it.

Macy had always had a secret fear that after you died, you didn't actually leave your body, but just stayed in your own rotting corpse for the rest of eternity. At least she now knew that wasn't the case.

The little girl bounced the ball again. This time it rolled away from her. Macy bent down and picked up the ball, holding it out for the girl. To anyone else, it would have appeared as if Macy was just looking at her own empty palm. The little girl slowly walked over, limping. When she stood up and faced Macy, it was easier to see the bruising around the girl's neck and the dark pattern where her shattered cheekbone was slightly sunken in. She smiled shyly at Macy—her two front teeth were broken—and reached out her hand to take the ball back.

When she first saw the girl, Macy had instantly recognized her from the newspaper, though she had forgotten her name. She felt bad about that. Someone should remember her name. Four years earlier, just after Christmas, the six-year-old girl was found dead in her parents' backyard. She was strangled and beaten, with a broken leg, the back of her head bashed in. The girl had been killed sometime during the night, and when they found her body the next morning it was covered in frost. Macy didn't read that part in the newspaper—she could see the white frost that coated the girl's hair and lashes. There was nothing to indicate that the parents had been involved in their daughter's death and there were no other suspects or leads. The case was never solved.

Macy wondered if the girl's parents had moved away, or if they still lived in that house where they could look out their window onto the small square of grass where their daughter's body had grown cold. What would Macy have done? Probably stayed, she figured, because that house at least still held the girls' memories. What would it be like if everyone could see ghosts? What if all ghosts just stayed after they died and you could continue that final conversation? If everyone could just keep going and going, like the Energizer Bunny . . .

In a perfect world Macy would have asked the little girl who had killed her and gone triumphantly to the police or the parents with the information. Macy would have been a hero and seeing her killer brought to justice would have let the girl's ghost rest in peace. But the world was anything but perfect, and the girl was a shadow of her living self. Just the image of the sun on the back of your eyes after you've already looked away from the sky. Dom had explained that these kinds of ghosts couldn't tell you anything—they weren't complete. They weren't strong enough to keep their identity whole. Just an afterimage. An echo. Macy had started using that term in her head for the weak ghosts: echoes.

Instead of giving the ball back to the girl, Macy placed her other hand on top of her head. Even through the silk glove Macy could feel the blood oozing from the back of the child's head. She closed her eyes, drawing in a deep breath. Macy pictured a dandelion gone to seed—a hundred stars forming their own perfectly round galaxy. She held the flower up to her lips, then blew. The stars scattered in all directions, dissolving across the sky. Macy opened her eyes and the girl was gone.

Since the Door opened five weeks earlier, Macy had personally taken care of more than thirty ghosts. She was talented, even Sam agreed. It had come easily to Macy after the first terrifying attempt in the burning gym. But it wasn't something she got used to—not even as her mind learned how to latch onto the ghosts like a key turning in a lock. Children were the worst. Macy wanted to tell them that it would be okay—that she was sending them somewhere so much better. Heaven, maybe. But she didn't know that. All Macy knew was that she couldn't look at that broken girl for another minute. Anything had to be better than her fractured cheek and lost, hollow eyes.

Macy brushed off her hands, even though there was nothing on them. Her parents were still talking to the funeral director. She could just hear the soft flow of their voices from where they stood by the front door, but not actual words.

An abandoned funeral pamphlet lay on the pew beside her. Nick's face was on the cover, staring up at the wooden beams of the church ceiling. Their mother had chosen his senior picture—not his best—and he had a toothy, open-mouthed smile. Nick hadn't liked that picture but Macy did. It made her brother look like he was about to say something. He wore a suit and tie and his brown hair was brushed back with gel, making him look older than eighteen.

Looking at the picture, Macy realized that it was as old as he was ever going to get. At some point Macy was going to catch up to him and then keep getting older and older until she was wrinkled with saggy boobs and cankles. And he would still look like that. He would be eighteen forever.

For the thousandth time, Macy wondered why her brother's ghost hadn't come back. What did it take? Didn't slamming your car into a tree qualify as having unresolved issues? But Dom had said that there might not be any reason to it. The legend that ghosts still had work left to do on earth before they could "move on" might be all wrong. And shouldn't she wish that her brother was at peace? Shouldn't she hope he was in heaven, if that existed? But the truth was that Macy just wanted to see him again. Not as he was in his last moments—with his face torn up and his arm missing. She wanted him to come back whole.

Macy took out her phone. No messages. You'd have to be a real jackass to text a girl during her brother's funeral, but Macy hadn't seen Dominick all weekend, and she kind of hoped that he had sent her something. Even just a quick "hi." Claire and Jackson had come to the funeral, but she didn't invite Trev, Sam, or Dominick. It wasn't really something you invited someone to. *Hey, I'm throwing this rad party on Sunday and BTW, it's my dead brother's funeral.* Besides, part of her worried that if they were at the church and her brother's ghost appeared, they might kill him before she had a chance to talk to him.

With other ghosts she could think of it as "taking care" of them, but not when it came to her brother. It would be like watching him die all over again.

She wondered what Dom was doing. He had missed a lot of school after the fire. To be honest everyone had. They shut the whole school down for two weeks while they investigated how the fire started. It had rained the entire time.

September was sometimes beautiful in Grey Hills: day after day of blue sky before fall settled in for good and brought dead leaves and a constant drizzle. Not this year. It was as though the sky itself was mourning the two dead students. Cassandra Decker. Sean Howard. A senior and a junior—dead from third-degree burns and smoke inhalation. A few other students had horrible burns—one boy went blind. One senior girl had actually tried to kill herself because she felt so guilty about the whole thing, but she didn't take enough pills and just got really sick. Macy doubted that she really wanted to die—the girl probably needed to *do something* in the face of so much loss. Macy understood how that felt.

Although the authorities never found a source for the fire, everyone blamed the senior prank. The most surprising part of the fire was how quickly it was put out and how little damage was actually done to the school. Just like the kitchen fire, there had been a lot of smoke damage, but the structure itself was mostly unharmed.

Mr. Fitch was fired and then he immediately left town. He didn't even sell his house first. They needed to blame someone, and it was Mr. Fitch who had argued that they go ahead with the Lock In, even after the lunch lady died. Macy sometimes wondered if Mr. Fitch really *did* have something to do with it and had been working with Lorna all along. But short of tracking down Mr. Fitch and questioning him as Sam had suggested more than once—and she always held up air quotes when she said "question"—they really had no way to find out. Lorna, after all, was gone for good.

The families of the two students who died had their own funerals. It felt strange to go ahead with Nick's funeral after all that time, as if her own loss wasn't as valid as that of the burned students' parents and siblings. The students were the elite dead, while Nick's death was old news by the time her parents finally got around to actually having his funeral.

Some students had shown up, including Nick's closest friends, and Claire and Jackson of course. Macy suspected that most of the student body was sick to death, so to speak, of funerals. And Nick had already graduated so most of the underclassmen hadn't really known him. He'd been in that *in-between* point of his life—out of high school, but not yet in college. Just kind of waiting for his life to begin.

Another reason for the low turnout was that the timing wasn't great. Macy's mom had decided that Nick's funeral would be a morning service, because mornings always had "so much promise." Macy wanted to tell her Mom that it was a good thing Nick didn't have to go, because he would probably have slept through it. Nine a.m. would have been way too early. But Macy didn't say that. Her dad would have laughed, but her mom didn't understand that kind of humor.

When the service ended at ten thirty, Macy was supposed to go back home with her mom and dad and have brunch with her grandparents. Nick would have rolled his eyes at the idea of a funeral brunch. He didn't even believe in brunch as a concept. The first meal of the day was breakfast, period. Brunch was for chicks who wanted to sit around and gossip. Did anyone even say "chicks" anymore? Like women were baby farm animals or something? But that's how Nick talked.

Macy stood by her mom for a few minutes while she kept going on and on to the funeral director about the flowers she wanted to donate to the hospital.

"Give them to a new mother—fill her room with flowers." Her mom's voice shook as she spoke, and she still held that box of tissues, slightly crushing it with her grip.

Her mom was a few inches taller than Macy, with dyed brown hair. It had gone mostly gray when she was only twenty-three and Macy had recently begun staring at her own roots in the mirror, searching for strands of silver. She had once read that the gene for hair loss came from your mother's father—and her mom's dad was bald—but she didn't know about gray hair. That was another thing Nick didn't have to put up with. He wouldn't have to go bald at forty-five like their grandpa.

The funeral director nodded. "Of course, Mrs. Pierce. That's a lovely idea."

"It's what Nick would have wanted," her mom said, dabbing her eyes.

Macy almost snorted at the idea of Nick ever having a single thought about the disposal of a room full of white lilies. The flowers were very strong smelling and were starting to make Macy's eyes water. What new mother would want death flowers in her room?

Her dad stood beside his wife, but didn't say anything. With his lost expression and patches of stubble on his neck that he had overlooked while shaving that morning, he resembled someone who had just woken up on a bus and hadn't yet figured out that he'd missed his stop.

Finally, when it looked like her mom was just going to keep bothering the funeral director, Macy gave a little *I'm-leaving* wave and walked out the front door. She would text her mom a little later and tell her that she went over to Claire's.

The thought of sitting through brunch with her weepy grandparents made her feel nauseous. They were staying another night so she'd see them at dinner.

Chapter Two

Dominick's house wasn't that far from the church—maybe ten blocks. Macy didn't have an umbrella, but the rain felt nice on her face. It was like walking through a cloud.

On the way to Dom's she saw three more ghosts. The first was just another echo—a middle-aged man who kept stepping out into the street and covering his head with his arms. Then he would vanish. He did this two times before Macy took care of him. Macy didn't even need to touch him. She just closed her eyes and imagined the man's body melting with the rain.

The second was another child—about eleven

years old. He sat on the sidewalk and looked up at Macy as she walked by. She might not have even known he was dead except for his hair—it wasn't wet, even in the rain. And his clothes looked old, like something you would see in a museum. Lace-up boots and a wool coat with wooden buttons. At a quick glance Macy couldn't tell what had killed him. He just sat with his chin in his hands and watched her walk by. When she tried to place her hand on his head, it just passed right through. She snatched her hand back as the boy frowned up at her.

Some of the ghosts were stronger than others—that was something Macy had learned in the past five weeks. The little girl in the church had been strong. Macy could have picked her up and held her battered body to her chest and rocked her. She could have carried her home. But she was still an echo, and when Macy willed the girl's body—her ghost—to disperse, it had been so easy. This boy was something less, just a true shadow. Macy couldn't even touch him. It was even easier than the middle-aged man. Sometimes taking care of ghosts was like sweeping up cobwebs.

The third ghost was hiding behind a tree just a block from Dominick's house. When she walked past, the ghost threw herself at Macy, grabbing her hair and pushing her down onto the sidewalk. Even though it all happened so fast, Macy recognized her—Andrea Ivers. Andrea had been a friend of one of Nick's girlfriends. She had OD'd three years earlier. They found her body in the backseat of a car. Her friends had left her there to "sleep it off" and she had choked on her own vomit.

The ghost had long, stringy blond hair and she smelled terrible—like stomach acid and beer. "Fucking bitch!" Andrea screamed in Macy's ear. She was on Macy's back, still holding her by the hair.

Macy struggled against the ghost, pushing herself up onto her hands and knees. "Get off!"

Macy hissed. Her knees stung from hitting the pavement and she was pretty sure her tights were ripped. They had cost twenty dollars and were the kind that sucked in your stomach and made you look skinny. Now they were ruined. *Bitch!*

Andrea pulled Macy's head back and laughed. "I know you," she said in a sing-song voice. "I *know* you."

Macy wanted to tell Andrea that she didn't know jack shit about her. That she was Nick's little sister and was only thirteen when Andrea died in the back of an old Toyota. But there was no point. Whoever the ghost thought she was, there was no talking her out of it. Ghosts were like cats—very single-minded.

Starting from the moment the ghost tackled her, it took Macy seven seconds to come up with a plan. She bet that Dominick or Sam would have already had a plan before a ghost jumped them, but she was still learning. And Trev might have been able to talk his way out of it. First, Macy let herself fall back onto her stomach. Her scalp screamed as she wrenched her head down too, taking Andrea with her. *Fuck, fuck!* She ground her fingertips into the pavement from the pain. Then, with Andrea unbalanced, Macy reached up with both hands and grabbed her nasty hair. Macy's burned hands stung as she pulled the ghost's hair as hard as she could, flipping her over the top of her head. Andrea landed hard on her back and let out a loud "ooph!" As if she had any breath in her lungs.

As fast as she could, Macy got to her knees and pulled her butterfly knife out of her dress pocket. She flipped the knife open with the flick of her wrist, then slammed the blade into Andrea's forehead. There wasn't any blood—that was the freaky part about stabbing a ghost. (Okay, *one* of the freaky parts. Freaky part number one was that you've just stabbed a fucking ghost). You might think it would be like when people are stabbed in the movies and blood spurted out of the wound like a lawn sprinkler. But ghosts didn't seem to bleed when she cut them. Andrea rolled her eyes up toward the blade, then let out a terrible scream. Macy covered her ears with her hands until the ghost disappeared.

Chapter Three

Sam was driving, which meant that when she came to a stop sign on the way out of town the car lurched and stalled. "Fucking . . . fucker," Sam muttered, grinding the stick into first gear. The car stuttered when she stepped on the gas, almost dying again. Jackson's seatbelt tightened across his chest as he was jerked back and forth and Trev groaned from the seat behind Sam. The car filled with the smell of burning clutch. Dom didn't say anything, for once, because he wasn't there. *Thank God.* Dom had stayed home because his shoulder was still healing, and sitting in the car while Sam learned how to drive a stick shift would probably have made him pop a stitch or something. Jackson didn't miss Dom's lectures, or the way he squinted his eyes disapprovingly whenever Jackson spoke. Plus it was Dom's car, and listening to Sam brutalize his clutch would probably have given the little guy an aneurysm.

The car finally sped forward, skidding for a moment on the wet road. "You drive like a psycho," Trev said, kicking the back of Sam's seat.

"Can *you* work a stick?" Jackson asked Trev.

Trev laughed like Jackson had made a joke and Sam snorted.

"Sure," Trev answered. "I'm a pro."

Jackson turned back to Sam and asked, "Then why don't *you* know how?" Sam was wearing her hair up, and he noticed a tiny mole on the side of her neck, just above her collarbone. Or maybe it was just a really big freckle. He often wondered where else Sam had freckles.

"It's not like we're Siamese twins," Sam replied. "His boyfriend taught him."

"Oh." Jackson didn't realize Trev was gay. Macy had probably known immediately with that "gaydar" girls claimed to have, but she sure didn't tell him. *Thanks Mace.* Jackson tried to think of what he might have said in the past few weeks that would have made him sound like a homophobic jackass. He didn't think he was a homophobic jackass, but he never knew what kind of crap might have spilled out of his mouth. They were always talking about ghosts, so maybe it was fine. Now that he thought about it, he couldn't remember Trev ever hitting on Claire, which was the first thing guys usually did. Had Trev ever hit on Jackson?

Jackson glanced in the backseat. Trev gave him a cool, even smile, like he was daring Jackson to have a problem with this new information. In middle school, Jackson used to say that things were "gay"—like, taking a headshot in Halo was gay. Having to clean the cat litter was so gay. His mom would yell at him when he talked like that, as though he had said something really bad, like *fuck*, in front of his grandmother.

"You have a boyfriend?" Jackson asked.

"Nah," Trev said. "We broke up before we moved here. He's still in Texas."

"He was hot," Sam said, turning up the wipers. "I would've done him." The wipers made an annoying squeaking sound every time they swung to the right. *Squeak, kathump, squeak, kathump.* The rain was getting heavier and the view out Jackson's window was wet and gray. Everything outside of Grey Hills was crazy rural—like, cows and horses and little farmhouses. *Little House on the Prairie* shit. The road stretched up a long valley with wide pastures on either side. If it kept raining like this, the pastures would flood and it would look like you were driving up the middle of a huge flat lake.

"He was alright," Trev said. "Kind of clingy, actually."

"Amazing ass."

Jackson didn't want to listen to Sam talk about Trev's ex-boyfriend's ass, amazing or otherwise. He wanted to know what they were going to find at the lake about twenty miles out of town. He started punching at Dom's radio presets. Static. Had Dom really not set up his presets since moving to town? Weirdo.

"Here." Sam pressed the CD button. U2's "With or Without You" filled the car.

"No!" Trev yelled, covering his ears. "No more *Joshua Tree*!"

"I like it," Sam replied, turning the volume up even louder. She sang along, but Jackson couldn't really make out her voice over the sound of the car wheels on the wet road, the wipers, and Bono's soaring voice on the tinny speakers.

When Jackson had knocked on Sam's door that morning and told her about the old ghost story, he was about eighty percent sure that she would tell him not to waste her time. A man had murdered his wife with an axe, dumped her body in the lake, and hung himself from the rafters of a boathouse. Sometimes the man's ghost came back and drowned people. When he told her the story, Sam's eyes had lit up and she said, "When do we leave?"

Jackson had responded with, "How about right now?" because he needed to do *something* after sitting through Nick's funeral. He had been able to see the back of Macy's head during the service, but not her face. She probably didn't even know he was there. And Claire had been a mess, with tears running down her unusually makeup-free face. The whole thing had made Jackson restless and jumpy, like there were ants crawling in his blood.

As Sam kept driving—smoothly now that she could hang out in fifth gear—pasture eventually gave way to trees. The road was so dark it seemed like late afternoon instead of morning. It was hard to believe that the whole day was still ahead of them. The service had seemed to go on forever and trying not to cry was exhausting. Jackson felt a little bad for leaving right after the funeral, but Macy probably had family stuff to do. And, to be honest, he hated that church. It was the same one his mom had chosen when she planned her own funeral. Jackson's family didn't really go to church at all, but his mom thought it was a lovely building. He wondered if his mom had gone to her own funeral, and if so, was she disappointed?

"Turn here!" Jackson yelled over the music, pointing to a small road that peeled off to the left. He braced himself for Sam to take the turn too quickly, or kill the car, but she slowed and let the car gently roll onto the dirt road.

Trev leaned forward. "Good job!" he yelled in his sister's ear. "I didn't even throw up."

The road was in bad shape, with huge rain-filled potholes making the car tip to one side or almost bottom out. Jackson felt like he was in a leaking boat. The windows had started to fog up so Jackson rolled down his window and stuck his hand out.

He touched the dripping cedar branches as they passed.

"Now it's raining inside," Trev grumbled. "Wonderful." Ever since Sam had woken her brother up to come on their little adventure, Trev had been less than enthusiastic about the whole thing. With his hair sticking up and now a little frizzy from the rain, Jackson thought Trev resembled a cat who had just been given a bath.

"Just stay on the road, it goes all the way to the lake," Jackson yelled over the music.

Sam nodded, tapping the steering wheel with her fingertips. Jackson had never met anyone like Samantha Moss before—at least outside of a movie. Macy always said she hated those characters: the ones who show up partway through the movie acting all crazy, but were so hot the male characters fall in love with them immediately. She's the kind of girl who takes off her clothes and jumps in a fountain or hops on a train without knowing where it's going. Macy used to go on rants that those girls weren't real. They were some horny screenwriter's wet dream. Jackson thought that Macy would probably have hated Sam if she was in a movie. Hell, Macy probably kind of hated Sam in real life. Macy always acted weird around her—nervous or something.

After four more teeth-rattling miles, they arrived at Horseshoe Lake. Sam pulled off to the side of the road—there wasn't really much of a parking area—and turned off the car. The sudden silence made Jackson's ears fuzzy, like they were full of cotton.

The lake was named after its shape: wide and narrow with a horseshoe-like curve and a narrow piece of land that jutted out into the middle of the water. At the end of this little peninsula was an old, rotting boathouse. Fir trees and cedars surrounded the lake, making it feel like you were miles and miles from anything. They *were* miles from anything—Jackson was pretty sure that no one would be able to hear them scream. While he didn't really think that they'd find anything here, just thinking of the possibility gave him a pleasant chill down his spine, like watching a scary movie. Those were always his favorite kind.

The rain had eased up in the last few minutes. Rather than falling, it looked like the rain was just hovering in place as a thick mist.

"Okay . . . what's the plan?" Sam asked, looking back at her brother. Jackson was a little annoyed that she obviously didn't direct the question toward him. Maybe Jackson had an amazing plan. She didn't know. He didn't have a plan beyond driving to the lake, but that wasn't the point. He *could* have, and she didn't ask.

Trev started to draw something on the fogged glass. It was either a monster or a very improbable penis. "I think I've seen this one before. We split up, right? One of us checks out the creepy-ass shack. Someone else goes swimming—gotta be you, sis, since, you know, boobs. And maybe

Jackson wanders around the woods for a while until a tree stabs him in the throat?"

Sam ignored her brother and turned to Jackson. "I actually do think we should start with the building. Ghosts tend to stay in one place—somewhere they feel comfortable and safe. If there *is* a ghost here, I bet he'd want to be inside the shack."

"Boathouse," Jackson corrected, then blushed. "I mean, yeah. Okay, sure." Over the past few weeks Jackson had instituted a policy of agreeing with whatever Sam said. Do you want another beer? *Sure.* Do you want to ditch Trev and make out in the creepy-ass shack? *Whatever you say!*

As he got out of the car, Jackson suddenly wondered how Macy was doing. She popped into his head all the time, even when he just wanted to check out Sam's tight jeans as she walked toward the boathouse. It wasn't just Macy in general that he thought about, but specifically "Macy in his basement"—that afternoon at the beginning of summer. That shitty day. The memory was always with him, like a sticky, shameful film that clung to his skin. He thought about it all the time. Not the kiss exactly—and was it really even a kiss if only one person is doing the kissing? He thought about that look on her face. It wasn't just anger and it wasn't just pity—though her face was also full of both of those emotions. What he had seen in her eyes when he held her wrist for a moment too long was worse than anger or pity. It was disappointment.

Chapter Four

Macy knelt in the rain for a few minutes after the ghost vanished, waiting to see if she was going to cry. Her eyes burned, but she blinked back the tears and breathed deeply until she was under control. Then she stood up slowly, wincing as she straightened her skinned knee.

The trickle of blood that ran down her leg looked worse than it really was because of the rain. It reminded her of when she was eleven or twelve years old and always cut her legs shaving in the shower. The blood had pooled at her feet in rusty pink puddles before washing down the drain.

Macy pressed one of her wet gloves to her knee

and limped towards Dom's house. She hesitated when she got to the front door, then knocked.

It took a few tries before Dom opened the door. Macy's heart gave a little twist when she saw his sleep-rumpled hair and groggy eyes. "Hey," he said, blinking at her. "You're all wet." He was wearing a soft-looking white shirt and sweatpants. She must have woken him up.

"Yeah. It's raining."

He seemed to look past where she stood on the covered porch to the dripping lilac bush in the front yard. "Oh. You're right," he said.

Dom had been taking some serious pain meds as the hole in his shoulder slowly healed. Dom didn't like to talk about it, but Trev told Macy that the bullet had caused some nerve damage. Even if the actual wound was getting better, there was some pain that might never go away completely.

Macy was getting used to Dom's spaced-out, glossy eyes, but she didn't like it. She had come to rely on Dominick, out of all of them, to know what the hell was going on.

Macy walked past Dom and went straight to the kitchen. First she grabbed a paper towel to clean up her bloody leg. Then she took the knife out of her pocket and dropped it on the table. Dominick startled at the sound, then crossed his bare arms.

"Four," Macy said. "I just took out four ghosts. One in the church and three on the way here."

"I'm sorry," Dom said. He was always apologizing to her lately, like he was somehow to blame for everything. He had said he was sorry the other day when Macy spilled coffee on herself. Dom sometimes even apologized for the rain.

"I just . . . " Macy ran her hands through her wet hair. Her scalp was still tender from Andrea's attack. "When's it going to end? Is this just the way the world is now? Like, forever? Just ghosts and more ghosts?"

Dom finally seemed to wake up enough to

notice the state of Macy, with her ripped tights and skinned knee. "You okay?"

Macy sighed. "No. I mean, yes. I'm fine. A bitch ghost pulled my hair and pushed me down. And I took care of her. But no. It's not fine. This"—Macy held her hands up, gesturing to everything—"is not fine. Can we just live like this? Is this what it's always like, in the places you were before? The other Doors?"

Dom got Macy a glass of water and one for himself. He drank deeply and rubbed his eyes again.

She knew he didn't like being medicated, which meant the pain must have been really bad today, because he was trying to cut down on the pills.

"No, none of the Doors were like this. We called them Doors, but they were more like cracks. This Door—it's wide open. I've never seen anything like it."

"Have you found anything?" she asked. Dom was supposed to be researching a way to close the

Door. So far he had found a web series about a cat who could fit in all kinds of boxes, and a Russian cartoon about a girl and her pet bear, but nothing about how to keep ghosts from flooding Macy's town.

Macy wasn't even sure how Dom was supposed to be researching—did he just type "how to close a Door to Hell" into Google? Maybe she should try that herself.

"Not really. Maybe. I don't know." Dom yawned.

His breath wasn't great and Macy felt kind of bad for being annoyed that he wasn't finding answers. She wasn't the one who got shot.

Macy still had dreams about it sometimes—dreams that felt real because they were practically memories. Dom was bleeding and she tried to help lift him but her burned hands hurt so bad she almost threw up.

That part was real. The part that was only a dream was when the Door kept getting bigger and bigger until it swallowed them both like an exploding sun. That was when she always woke up—after it was too late, but before she actually saw what was on the other side of the Door.

Dom held his hand out to Macy. "Come on, I want to show you something."

Macy didn't take Dom's hand. Her burns still hurt, even after all those weeks. That's why she wore gloves—and because she didn't want her parents to know her palms were still covered in tender blisters.

Letting his empty hand drop, Dom led Macy up the stairs to his room. They usually sat around the kitchen table when they talked, and Trev and Sam always took up all the space in the room with their bickering.

"Hey, where are the twins?" Macy asked.

Dom glanced back at her. "They ran off somewhere with Jackson. They left about twenty minutes ago. He had a ghost he wanted to show them."

Macy could hear a slight twinge of bitterness in Dom's voice. She had grown used to Dom being a kind of ringleader for the trio. He couldn't enjoy being left behind.

Jackson must have come here right after the funeral. She didn't remember Jackson or Claire leaving, but she did recall seeing them near the back of the church with their families. She had spent most of the actual service watching the ghost of the girl, fascinated by the bows in her hair and how focused she was on her game of jacks.

"Jackson has a ghost?" Macy sat on the edge of Dom's bed, her stomach doing a silly little flip as the mattress sank beneath her.

Was it stupid to be shy about sitting on a boy's bed when she had just stabbed a ghost in the fore-head? Yes. Definitely.

Dom sat at the simple—probably Ikea—desk by the bed. He turned on his laptop. "You tell me. Something about a ghost by a lake? It drowns people?"

Macy had a vague memory about some ghost story Jackson told her when they were both about ten years old. It was a man who drowned people or killed people with an ax. She had always thought Jackson made it up. "Well, I'm pretty sure that all they'll find at Horseshoe Lake is water."

Dom nodded and just kept typing at his computer. He had an almost invisible shadow of stubble along his jaw. She wondered what his jaw would feel like against her lips.

Sometimes Macy worried that other people could read her mind and knew everything she was thinking all the time. Which meant, of course, that they would be able to hear her wondering if they could read her mind. That was the part that always freaked her out the most: that someone might know that *you knew* that they could read your mind. How awkward.

At the moment, however, Macy wouldn't have minded if Dom could hear what she was thinking because she didn't know how to say it out loud.

She could see the muscles in his back move ever so slightly as he typed.

She looked around the room. The walls were bare and the room was fairly clean—clothes in a corner hamper, and the throw rug on the hardwood floor looked freshly vacuumed. She could see what looked like boxers through the mesh of the hamper.

She had seen Nick's and Jackson's boxers strewn about their filthy rooms plenty of times, but seeing Dom's felt different, like she had peeled off the cover of a book.

His windows didn't have any curtains and she could see out over the bluffs to the hazy line where the clouds met the water.

"Where'd you get this house?" Macy hadn't asked that before. She had wondered about it, though—how these kids who were her age could afford a giant Victorian house.

"What?" Dom glanced up from his computer. "Oh, it's Trev's. His and Sam's. They bought it."

"Bought? Like, they own it? You're not renting? How is that possible?" Macy took in the walls around her, and the many rooms, and the roof that made up this great big house. It must have been worth a million dollars. Not that she really knew what houses cost—a million was always her go-to amount when anything was inconceivably expensive.

"They don't actually like to talk about it. They have some money. From . . . a settlement."

"Settlement?"

"Um." Dom looked uncomfortable. He ran his hand through his hair and winced as he moved his shoulder. "I'll let them tell you."

"Sure." Macy looked down at her skinned knee. She poked a finger through her torn leggings to the drying blood. It hurt, but she kept doing it without thinking, like picking at a hangnail. "Anyway, you were going to show me something?"

"Yeah." He turned his laptop towards her. The screen showed a news article about a serial killer in Arizona. A few years earlier someone had killed four women by slitting their throats, but he was never caught.

Macy just assumed the killer was a *he*. It happened right around Halloween, so they called the murderer the Halloween Killer. Clever.

Dom pointed at the article, actually pressing his finger on the screen. Macy hated it when people did that. She wanted to wipe the fingerprint off the screen with the fabric of her dress, but she resisted.

"This town had a Door too," Dom said. "But after these women died, the Door closed. I think it was a ritual."

"It says that?" Macy got up and leaned over his shoulder. "It mentions the Door?"

"No, of course not. But we had it marked on the map as a Door that just vanished. It's very odd for a Door to disappear, so I remembered it."

Macy tried to make sense of this new information. They already knew that a Door had closed before and didn't tell her? She decided to let that one go. There was so much she still didn't know about the trio.

"Okay," she said, "but now you think these murders had something to do with it?"

"Yeah. Slitting someone's throat is very ritualistic. Bloodletting, sacrifice . . . all that stuff. And they were all killed near the Door."

Macy shook her head. "That doesn't make any sense. Why would Lorna try to kill a ton of people to keep the Door closed if she could have just killed four people to close it later? That doesn't sound very efficient."

"I don't think we'll ever know what was going on in her head. Or what happened in the last fire. Not unless Lorna's ghost comes back for an interview. Maybe the fire was the only ritual she knew? She was obviously pretty scared about what would happen if the Door opened."

Macy remembered Lorna's face in the darkness—how devastated she looked when she knew she had failed. It was hard not to feel sorry for a terrified old woman, but Macy did her best. Just thinking about Lorna made Macy clench her teeth so hard that her jaw hurt.

Macy sat back down on the bed. Leaning over Dom's shoulder was starting to get uncomfortable. The she realized what he was actually showing her. "Wait, so you *do* know how to close it? The Door?"

Dom nodded, smiling at her. Then he shook his head. "No. I mean, *I* don't. But someone might. If I'm right and these killings were part of a ritual . . . "

"Someone? Are there others like you? Other people who hunt ghosts?"

Dom rubbed his shoulder, looking back to the computer. "Not exactly like us, but yeah—other people know about Doors. Other people can see ghosts. Is that what you're asking? How do you think I learned anything? Fucking trial and error?"

Macy frowned. Dom didn't usually raise his

voice at her. "Yeah, I guess. I just didn't think there were chatrooms and stuff."

Dom yawned and put his hand over his shoulder again. His eyes drooped. "Sorry, what'd you say?" He looked terrible.

Macy really wanted to know more about those other people and this possible ritual, but Dom was obviously fading. He'd let her know when he found something useful. She just had to trust him.

"Nothing. Come here." Macy got up and patted the now empty bed. "You should lay down. I'll go."

Dom laid down on top of the bed, but he took Macy's wrist before she could leave. "Wait," he said. His hand was warm and she could feel her pulse beating beneath his fingers.

Macy couldn't look him in the eye. "What?"

"Just . . . you can stay a little longer. If you want. You look tired, too." Dom scooted over so he was against the wall.

The bed was a twin, but there was just enough

room for two people. She took off her shoes and got on the bed next to Dom.

He put his arm over her waist and pulled her close.

Chapter Five

"You smell nice," he said into her hair, his words slurring a little with sleep. She didn't say that his sheets smelled a little sour like a sick room. She didn't say that her neck tingled where his breath touched her skin, and that she wanted him even closer—so close that there would be no difference between him and her. So close that she could read his mind.

Instead, she asked, "Where'd you grow up?"

He didn't answer right away. Macy started to think that he had fallen asleep because his breath was so even. She could feel his chest rise and fall against her back. Then, in a low whisper, he said,

"I guess San Francisco. That's when I still lived with my parents."

"What was it like?" she asked, though what she really wanted to know was what had happened to his parents. What had happened to him? What had made him this way?

Dom moved his hand up to her hip, his fingers pulling at the fabric of her dress in an absent sort of way. He probably didn't even realize he was doing it. "We had a lemon tree in our backyard and we lived at the top of a really big hill. San Francisco's supposed to be so foggy all the time, but I just remember that it was sunny. I remember lying on my back and looking up at the blue sky through the trees. I think it was somewhere in the Mission district, but I don't really know. I was seven."

Macy held her breath, as though any sound—any distraction—would make him stop.

"I don't know why my sister was out that night. She was fourteen. When I was seven that seemed so old. My parents should have known where she was. How could they not have known? It's like the one job a parent has—keep your child safe. But they didn't know where she was and they didn't realize when she didn't come home that night. Someone found her three days later in an alley. The police thought she had been dead for about twelve hours, which meant there were two full days when she was still alive—and whatever they did to her, she could still feel it. She knew it was happening." Dom took a deep, shaky breath, like he had just surfaced from beneath the water. He let it out slowly while Macy tried to figure out what to say.

"That's horrible." Macy took his hand off her hip and held it to her stomach, wincing at the pressure against the palm of her hand. She could feel the soft hair of his arm against the skin of her own arm.

Dom had his other hand in her hair, pulling it away from her shoulder. "Yeah. It sucked." He kind of laughed, but there was no humor in it. "I didn't really know what was happening at first. At seven, you actually realize a lot more than people think. I knew she was dead. I knew I'd never see her again. I knew what it meant when someone was murdered—that a bad person had killed her. But they tried to keep the worst of it from me. If my sister hadn't come back, I might never have known."

"You saw her? Her ghost?" Dom's finger's grazed her neck and Macy tried not to shiver.

"She was the first ghost I ever saw. I thought I was dreaming because I knew she was dead. And dead people didn't ever come back to visit. My mom kept explaining that to me, like I wouldn't understand if she didn't keep telling me over and over again. She even compared it to when our dog was hit by a car. As if Fido splattered all over the fucking road was at all the same as my sister."

"You actually had a dog name Fido?" Macy winced at her question. *Yeah, 'cause that was the important part of the story.*

"Nah. I don't remember his name. I'm sure it was clever though. A character out of a book or some mythological reference. My parents always thought they were so fucking clever. Maybe it *was* Fido. They would have actually loved that— thought it was ironic or something. Don't you sometimes wish that pets would come back instead of people? Puppies and hamsters following us around? Little poodle ghosts?"

Macy gave a little laugh, but she didn't want Dom to get sidetracked. And she actually thought that ghost poodles would be fucking creepy. She asked, "What happened? When you saw your sister, I mean?"

"She came to see me after I was tucked into bed. Like I said, at first I thought I was dreaming. She would talk to me just like I'm talking to you. Just like she was really there. But she didn't look right. It was her eyes, to start with. She wouldn't open her eyes. Josefina. That was her name. Josie. She would brush her cold hands across my face, and kneel on the side of my bed. She would sing to me sometimes. Songs from the radio or lullabies our mom used to sing. But she would always get upset if *I* talked to *her*, because I just wanted to ask questions. *Wasn't she dead? Was she a ghost?* That kind of thing. She would put her hands over my mouth and shush me. It was always dark, so I didn't see the worst of it until one night when I got out of bed and pushed past her. I turned on the light.

"My sister's face had been cut. Long lines from the top of her forehead down to her chin. There was blood under her eyes and she wouldn't open them. Couldn't open them. She couldn't see, to know the light was on. That's something I still wonder about. Why couldn't her ghost see? Even if they cut out her eyes when she was alive . . . " Macy dug her fingers into Dom's hand and her fingertips stung. "Why couldn't she see after she died? Isn't death supposed to be this great release?

Isn't it supposed to free you from pain? From suffering? Why couldn't my sister see?"

"Oh, Dom." Macy had been biting her cheek. She made herself stop and ran her tongue over the skin inside her mouth. She could feel the rough imprint her teeth had left. It tasted like blood.

"I didn't know what I was doing. I saw her like that—all of it. The raw red lines on her wrists where she had been tied up. The cuts on her arms and legs. I didn't want to see her like that. I wanted her to go away. I put out my hands and screamed. I closed my eyes and I used the trick my dad had taught me, for when I was afraid of a monster in my room. I was supposed to imagine that the monster was a snowman in the summer and it was melting. I don't know if my dad made that up or if he read about it in some parenting book. Probably the book . . .

"So I imagined my sister melting. And I felt it—you know what I mean. I felt her, in my head. And then she was gone. I did that to her."

Macy shook her head against the pillow. "You didn't know what you were doing. You wouldn't have . . . I know you didn't mean it."

"But the thing is, if she came back here today, and I know what I know now, I think I would still do it." Dom pushed away from Macy so he was laying on his back. His voice was getting softer and slower. "She didn't deserve to be that way. She couldn't even see me. And her face . . . I think I would do it again."

Macy shook her head. "I don't believe you." Once again Macy pictured her brother as he was in his senior picture, with his stupid smile and his hair brushed back off his forehead. Not as he was in the hospital. Never that.

When Dom didn't answer, Macy turned to look at him. His eyes were closed and his arm was flung above his head at an awkward angle. "Dom?" she whispered, but he didn't move. She sat up carefully, then leaned over him. Macy imagined herself kissing his mouth, gently, like he was an enchanted prince from a fairy tale. Instead she pressed her lips to the side of his mouth where his skin was darkened with stubble. Her kiss was so soft that she barely touched him. But she still felt him on her lips as she went down the creaky stairs and walked out the front door into the rain.

Chapter Six

The boathouse looked like something out of a horror movie. Moss covered the decaying roof, and the sides were a grayish green. The door was missing so the front looked like a huge, gaping mouth.

Jackson had first read about the dead man in a newspaper that his dad left out on the coffee table. He was nine or ten and usually just grabbed the comics. That day, however, the headline caught his attention: FOUR BODIES FOUND AT HORSESHOE LAKE. They didn't include a picture of the man's body hanging from the low rafters of the boathouse, but they did have a picture of the lake—black and white and grainy. Apparently the fall wasn't enough to break the man's neck, so he had probably strangled to death. The reporter had described the body: he was "severely decomposed" to such an extent that his body had come loose from his head and lay in a messy heap on the floor.

They found his wife's body rotting and bloated in the shallows. Both husband and wife had been dead for a few weeks. Jackson had wondered at the time if the wife was naked, but it didn't say in the article. He imagined her body surfacing, gray and leathery, like one of those manatees in the Everglades. Jackson didn't actually know what a dead body looked like, but he knew exactly what a manatee looked like because they had read a book about them in fifth grade.

The strangest part of the article was the second couple. They had only been dead for a few days and they were both drowned. No sign of a struggle— like they had each held their own heads under the water and breathed in the greenish, murky lake water that was contaminated with the decomposing body of the dead woman. Disgusting.

Jackson had thought about that story for years, wondering what had actually happened. It was a mystery that the town wanted to forget. Grey Hills already had the Fire, the specters of the burned students looming over it. It didn't need a haunted lake as well. The man who hung himself and murdered his wife were both older people. They had no children and had lived outside of town in a crappy mobile home in the woods. They were easy to forget.

The drowned couple was younger, in their early twenties. Just out of college and traveling. A tragic accident, but they had no family nearby to miss them. When Jackson told Macy the story, he had tried to tell it the way he thought about it—the way he dreamed about it. That man climbing down from his rope and wading into the water. He must have pulled the man under the water first, Jackson thought, and then the woman.

That's how it usually worked in scary movies—the women tended to die last.

Sam walked faster than Jackson, and he had to kind of half-jog to keep up. "In a hurry?" he called to her.

"It's fucking raining. Let's just get this over with." But Sam was grinning. She slowed down a little and let Jackson catch up. Trev had hardly moved from the car. He stood grimacing down at the sticky muck along the shore.

"Hurry up!" Sam yelled to her brother. "You're slow as fuck."

"This place smells like shit," Trev called back. "And yes, let's all just run into the haunted shed. Great fucking idea."

When they reached the boathouse they all peered in one of the broken windows. The building was big enough for two or three smallish boats—canoes or rowboats—to fit side by side. But there weren't any boats, just some broken beer bottles and a few empty milk crates off to one side.

"See anything?" Jackson asked, because he had to. He couldn't see anything ghostly himself.

Sam shook her head. "Nah, empty."

Jackson didn't know why he couldn't see ghosts the way the others did. Dom had always said there were levels of sight, but Jackson's level seemed like the ground floor. Macy could see things that even Dom couldn't—like that fucked-up ghost with the goggles—but Jackson couldn't see jack shit. He couldn't even really see the Door, just a sort of wavy, mirage-thing that would disappear if he looked at it straight on. And ghosts were usually completely invisible. He had seen something like fire at school a few times. That first day of school, when Macy had seen the ghost of a teacher burning, Jackson had seen flames appear out of nowhere—licking the air around the front of the classroom for a few seconds before they vanished. But ever since the Door opened and the town was just flooded with an assload of ghosts, he couldn't really see anything. He would stare toward a ghost that the others said they could see and maybe he would see something that looked like waves of heat rising off the cement—if he were lucky. Once he felt a shiver of cold when he was walking down the street and Macy told him he'd just passed through a ghost. *Thanks for the heads up, Mace. Fuck.* Jackson hated it. If someone had poured out this "superpower" out of a bottle, then all Jackson had gotten was the spit-filled backwash at the end.

They walked to the lake side of the boathouse. Trev was right, the lake did smell kind of nasty. Jackson stepped in some green duck shit and tried to wipe off his shoes on the patchy, wet grass. The smell reminded Jackson of dead fish and rotting grass clippings left out too long in the yard. Sam went into the boathouse first, holding a big flashlight over her head like she thought she was a cop from a movie.

"Cozy," Trev said, covering his nose with his sleeve. "We could summer here."

Jackson gestured to the thick beams that ran

along the ceiling. "He must have hung himself there."

Sam pointed the light to the rafters. They startled a small bird. It flapped its wings, but didn't fly away. "I don't know. I'm just not feeling it." Spider webs caught the light, and Jackson ducked lower to avoid them.

"Sorry." Jackson mumbled. She shouldn't have been this disappointed. Did he actually want to find a murderous ghost? "I thought it was worth a look."

"No prob." Sam smiled at Jackson. "I needed an excuse to practice a stick anyway."

"That's what she said," Trev chimed in.

Sam groaned. "Yes. I'm a girl. And that *is* what I said."

Trev grabbed the flashlight out of Sam's hands. He held it up under his chin. "I vant to suck your bluuud!" He wasn't holding it right, so the beam of light went right into Sam's eyes.

"Idiot," Sam hissed. She turned and left the

boathouse. Jackson could never tell when Sam was going to laugh at something her brother did or get all bitchy about it. She kind of scared the shit out of him most of the time.

Jackson went after her, catching up to her by the edge of the water. "So, what next?"

Sam picked up a twig and threw it into the lake. "How exactly does this ghost kill people? In the story?"

"Well, like I said, everyone drowned." After that first young couple died, three more people drowned in the lake. The drownings happened years apart and could easily have been accidents. One man was fishing by himself. When he didn't come to work the next day, a friend came out to the lake to check on him. He was found floating in the lake beside his boat, along with several empty beer cans. The authorities thought it was pretty obvious how the man died—drinking while operating a motor vehicle.

The two most recent deaths were another young

couple. A woman and her boyfriend were visiting the area from Portland. Again, it was a case of drowning with no signs of a struggle—nothing under the fingernails, no defensive wounds on the arms. Nothing to suggest that it wasn't just a terrible accident.

"Well, I say we lure the fucker out." Sam took off her raincoat and flung it at her brother who was still standing in the boathouse out of the rain. Trev didn't make a move to catch it and the coat fell into the lakeside muck. Sam rolled her eyes at her brother.

Then she took off her shirt.

Jackson swallowed and looked down at his feet. "What are you . . . ?"

"It's just a swimsuit." She slipped off her shoes, shimmied out of her jeans, and stood at the lake's edge in a very sporty blue-and-white two-piece. The top resembled a sports bra and the bottoms looked like tight shorts. She reminded Jackson of one of those Olympic beach volleyball players.

"Let's see if he takes the bait," Sam said. Then, before Jackson really had time to process anything beyond Sam taking off her shirt, she ran into the water. She shrieked at the cold and laughed as she sucked in her breath.

"What the fuck?!" Trev shouted after picking up her raincoat. "You know I was joking earlier? About you swimming? I know, it's kind of hard to tell when I'm joking since I'm usually so very serious."

"Water's great!" Sam called back to them. She was waist-deep, with her arms crossed over her chest. It had to be freezing. Sam was kind of far away to really tell, but Jackson thought her lips were turning purple.

Jackson had often imagined Sam taking off her clothes, but it had never involved her splashing around in a slimy, greenish lake that was full of duck shit.

"Don't get swimmer's itch!" Trev yelled, while his sister called out, "Come on in!"

Jackson's disappointment at not finding the ghost quickly vanished as he took off his shirt and shoes and then splashed his way to Sam.

"Shit, fuck!" Jackson yelped. The cold water hit him like a punch to the gut, sucking the breath out of him. But Sam was beautiful, even in the murky water. Some kind of water-weed was caught in her hair and she looked like a mermaid. The kind that eats people.

Trev had stepped out of the boathouse and was holding Sam's coat above his head like a cape. "You're both going to catch pneumonia and die, and then your ghosts are going to haunt me," he said. "I'll be the only one who can see you, but I'll ignore you. How'll you like that? It'll be like an episode of the fucking *Twilight Zone*."

"Dom and Macy could see us!" Jackson called back.

"But they'll be too busy doin' it like rabbits to care," Trev replied.

Jackson didn't really know what was going on

with Dom and Macy. They were always looking at each other with those stupid googly eyes, and it was really annoying. Dom hardly knew Macy, but he was always talking to her in this hushed voice like they were the only two people in the room. But as far as Jackson knew, nothing had really happened. Even if Macy didn't want to tell him, Claire would probably have let him know whether he asked her or not. Claire didn't really have a filter.

Jackson dove under the freezing water, instantly regretting it as the lake water went up his nose. He sputtered back to the surface and looked to see if Sam noticed him flailing around like an idiot. She wasn't there.

Chapter Seven

"Sam?" Jackson called out. "Sam?"

"Fuck!" Trev threw down his sister's coat and started wading into the water. He didn't even stop to take off his shoes. "Do you see her?"

Jackson swung around wildly. They had gone out deeper before she vanished, and the water was about up to his chest . . . which meant that it was probably up to Sam's chin. She was pretty tall for a girl, but not as tall as him. "I can't see her. I can't . . . " Then Jackson saw some strands of red hair floating near the surface like algae. "There!" He and Trev swam towards her. Trev, it turned out, was the better swimmer. He glided through the water like a fucking otter and then dove down. Trev must have been trying to pull his sister up, but it looked like she was caught on something. There was thrashing beneath the surface of the lake and it reminded Jackson of those nature videos of alligators, where they catch their prey in the water and spin and spin until they drown the victim.

"I see him," Trev gasped when he came up to take a breath. "Fucker has her feet. I'm going back down." He disappeared with another splash.

Jackson stood perfectly still in the disgusting water, his feet sinking slightly into the grainy muck. His nose still hurt from snorting in water and he had no idea what to do. He waited for three heartbeats for the twins to come back to the surface. But they were just shadows struggling beneath the water.

It was pouring by then, and the rain pocked the surface of the lake. Taking a deep breath, Jackson dove back under. He made himself open his eyes. They stung and he could barely see through the silt that Trev and Sam were churning up. He was probably going to get eye herpes or something from this shit. Jackson could just make out Sam's bare arms and legs and he swam towards them. Trev had his hands under Sam's armpits and was trying to pull her away from whatever had her legs. Sam was kicking and struggling, her face covered by a cloud of her long red hair.

Jackson swam for Sam's feet. He wished he had a harpoon or a trident like Ariel's dad in *The Little Mermaid*. That's who Sam looked like—Ariel. Not that it mattered right now. What he needed was something pointy, like a long stick, so he could stab the ghost (that he couldn't even fucking see) from a safe distance. But all he had were his hands. What would Macy do? Several times she had tried to explain to Jackson how she got rid of ghosts. Macy said that she let her mind take hold of them. She could feel what held them together, what kept them—their bodies?—from flying into a million little pieces. Then she pulled them apart. It made no fucking sense to Jackson, but he needed to try something.

Jackson put his hands on Sam's jerking legs. They were slimy and kept slipping from his grip. He thought that if the ghost had a hold of Sam's legs, then he could find the ghost by running his hand down to her feet. It wasn't a good plan, but Jackson had no other ideas at the moment. Trev had gone up for another breath and Jackson could hear the muted sound of him yelling.

Sam had stopped kicking and seemed to float limply. Trev was still tugging on her arms, but her legs were clearly being pulled down towards the mucky bottom. Jackson tried grabbing at the area beneath Sam, but he only felt water and stringy weeds. Soon he would need to take a breath. He could feel his lungs aching even as his teeth chattered from the cold. He tried pulling on Sam's legs himself, but she was stuck fast. Jackson stood up, pushing his face out of the water and sucking in air. Trev had his head above the water, still pulling on his sister.

"Do you see him?" Jackson gasped, his mouth barely working.

"Fucker's down there. I'm not strong enough. We need Dom." Jackson could barely understand Trev through his chattering teeth. Trev's wet hair was plastered to his forehead, and his lips looked blue. Jackson had never seen Trevor Moss like this—with eyes wide and terrified.

"Shit," Jackson said, then took another deep breath. He dove down again and nearly poked his eye out on an algae-covered branch. *Perfect!* He broke off the sharp end of the branch, cutting his palm in the process. It stung, but he tried to ignore the pain and focus on what he held in his hands. Now he had a foot-long, stabby . . . thing. A spear.

The water around his face clouded even more with his own blood and he could feel vomit coming up his nose. Jackson stared at Sam's limp feet. He held his stinging, twitching eyes open, willing himself to see something—anything. He tried to be Macy, to think with her brain. What would she see?

Finally, he saw—not a person exactly—but a shimmery, greenish smudge. It could have been anything, maybe the light from the sun finally breaking through the rain clouds, or just a patch of different colored algae. But it wasn't. It was Jackson's smudge. His ghost.

Jackson put his hand on Sam's cold, slippery ankle and stabbed the water just below her foot. He imagined that he was popping a balloon and all the air was going to shoot out in a jet of bubbles. He imagined a great white shark tearing through a school of fish, making them scatter.

Jackson thought he heard a scream, only it didn't sound muffled by the water. It was close and angry. It sounded like a man. Then Sam's foot slipped through his hand. Jackson resurfaced to find Trev holding Sam against his chest, swimming them both to shore.

Sam had been under the water for two minutes and fifty-eight seconds. It had felt like an hour to Jackson, but Trev had started counting the moment his sister's head vanished beneath the lake. He told this to Jackson on the drive home while Sam lay in the backseat with her head on Trev's lap, shivering and wrapped in the extra blankets that Dom kept in the trunk of his car.

When Trev first pulled his sister onto the shore, Sam wasn't breathing. Jackson was about to start CPR—he wasn't certified or anything, but he had seen plenty of movies and thought he knew the basics—when Trev pushed him aside. Trev turned Sam onto her side and pounded on her back until lake water poured out of her mouth and nose. She coughed and coughed, curling around herself. Jackson would never have said it out loud, but with greenish slime sticking to her chin, Sam looked like something that had already started to decompose.

"You stupid . . ." Trev murmured, lying down and wrapping himself around her. "Stupid, fucking . . ."

Sam coughed some more, hacking and spitting out more lake muck. Then she grinned a freaky, teeth-chattering grin. "Did it work?"

"What?" Jackson was on his hands and knees in front her, ready to do something—anything—if she needed him.

"Did you get him?" Sam's freckles stood out on her bloodless face. She tried to lift a hand, probably to brush her hair out of her eyes, but Trev had pinned her arms to her side in his embrace. Jackson moved the strand of hair for her.

"Yeah. I think so." Jackson felt himself grin too, though his face was almost too numb to feel it.

Trev glared at him. "Your fucking ghost." With Trev's face mostly buried in the back of Sam's neck, Jackson could barely hear him. "You two . . . I make the plans from now on. Stupid . . . fucking . . ."

Sam coughed, spit out more lake water, then she struggled against her brother until he helped her sit up. "So," Sam said between coughs. "When are we . . . doing this . . . again?"

Chapter Eight

After Macy left Dom's house she went straight to the Door. Macy didn't really plan it, she just started walking. It wasn't just Nick's funeral, it was his birthday. He would have been nineteen today and he probably would have been at college. She wouldn't have even seen him today anyway if he was still alive. Nick didn't like to talk on the phone, but she still could have called him and sung the happy birthday song in the little chipmunk voice that she always did to make him laugh. The University of Washington wasn't that far—she and her parents might have taken the ferry to Seattle for the day and gone out to dinner with Nick. They could have gotten Indian food because that was Nick's favorite, and Macy would have ordered the garlic naan and a big mug of chai with her dinner.

Or she and all her friends might be dead. Because if Nick hadn't died, Macy wouldn't be able to see ghosts. She wouldn't have been able to stop Lorna from burning down the school. Maybe Dom could have done it—but he never actually saw the ghost that started the fires. Macy often wondered about that—why she was the only one who could see the man in the goggles.

Macy could get to the Door from the school grounds, but she preferred to go a few blocks past the school and take a little path through the woods. That way you didn't have to climb over the fence. She wasn't the only one who walked around in the woods behind the school. She was always finding beer bottles and old crumpled packs of cigarettes. There were lots of little paths back there and you could even cut through the woods and take a trail down to the beach below. It was quite steep, though, and wasn't really an official trail. It looked pretty dangerous. Once Macy had taken the wrong path back there and found an old La-Z-Boy recliner that someone had hauled into the woods. It was soaked from the rain and had a big rip along the headrest. Macy wasn't sure if this was an alternative to hauling it to the dump or if someone actually sat in it from time to time.

It only took a few minutes from the road using one of the paths. She had been there so many times that her feet knew the steps by heart. When she got to the Door, Macy stopped and crouched down among the blackberry vines. They caught on her tights, tearing more long runs in the black fabric. They were ruined anyway, so what the hell. Rain dripped off the edge of her hood and splattered onto her knee. She shivered, watching the light from the Door throb and flicker. It was almost beautiful, but it was also terrible, like a TV set to the wrong ratio or color.

Almost every single day since the Door opened, Macy had come here and watched the ghosts come through. At first they came out quickly—shadows that seemed to stretch their way out of the Door like those blobs in a lava lamp. They would press against the Door as if there was some kind of barrier, and the pulsing light would bulge and bend outward until they broke through. It was almost like the ghosts were being born. That's what Macy tried to explain to Jackson because he couldn't see it the way she could. He said that if he squinted and looked out of the corner of his eye he could see a glimmer. That was all.

Once a ghost broke free it tended to do one of several things. Some of them ran—fleeing through trees and brambles and off into the distance. Andrea's ghost had probably been one of the runners. Other ghosts just vanished. Macy wondered where they went. Could ghosts wish themselves back to the houses they had lived in when they were alive or to a favorite coffee shop?

Or maybe it wasn't a place. Perhaps they wished themselves close to the one they loved when they were alive.

Or maybe they simply dissolved like the burned lunch lady. When she realized she was dead, it looked like she had just faded away. Dom said she wasn't one of the ghosts that lingered, but where did she go? Did the ghosts who vanished right after they died just go to the other side of the Door? Could they still come back?

Some ghosts stopped once they came through the door. They looked around with bewildered expressions, like sleepwalkers who had just awoken and found themselves far from their beds. Macy took care of these ghosts. It wasn't hard—these ghosts all felt like echoes, just wisps that scattered as soon as Macy imagined a dry leaf crumbling in her hand, or a sandcastle melting in the waves.

Today, as she stared into the glow of the Door and watched it waver and billow like a sheet caught in the wind, Macy wondered if it went the other way. Could a living person go through the Door? What would happen? Would you become a ghost yourself? This wasn't a new thought. Macy wondered about this every time she came here and watched the Door. Could you actually go into that mysterious place? But this time, as she thought about what lay on the other side of the Door, Macy decided to try something. She reached into her pocket and took out a quarter. She pressed her thumb against the dead president's face and ran her fingernail along the edge. Then she threw it at the door.

Light rippled as the quarter passed through and the Door seemed to bend inward. There was a strange smell, like burning plastic or hair. Then the coin was gone. Macy got up and looked on the other side of the Door, but realized that even had the quarter passed through to the other side and back out into the woods, it would be nearly impossible to find in the dead leaves and black-berry vines. And what if she did find a quarter?

How could she know for sure that it was her quarter?

"Fuck." Macy whispered the word, even though there was no one around to hear her. She would have to plan this out a little better next time she tried to test the Door. If there was a next time.

Macy got down on her hands and knees and felt with the palms of her hands, but couldn't feel the quarter. Part of her—a very small part—wanted to run into the Door and see what would happen. It was the same part of her that wondered what it would be like to drink Drano or put her hand in a moving fan. It didn't mean she was going to do it. But she couldn't help what thoughts went through her head.

As she searched for the coin, the Door began to move. Ghosts always came out of the side closest to the school. Macy was crouched on the other side, still feeling around for the quarter. As the Door bulged away from her, she froze. She had never witnessed a ghost coming out of the door from the other side before. The Door was slightly see-through, and she watched the trees distort and ripple on the other side.

Macy pulled her knife out of her pocket and flipped it open. When she had to stab a ghost to focus her energy, she'd always done it up close—actually pushing the blade into the ghost. She'd never thrown it before and she wondered if that was even possible. Could you take care of a ghost by throwing a knife at it or by shooting it with a gun? Or did a person's hand have to be touching the weapon for it to work? Macy had a lot of questions about ghost combat and ghosts in general, but Dom didn't always have enough answers.

When the ghost stepped through the Door, he didn't run. She could see enough through the Door to tell that it was a guy. He looked so familiar—tall, with thick hair. Something about the shape of his shoulders made her cry out, "Nick?"

She bit her cheek where it was already bloody and ragged. That was so stupid, saying Nick's name. But when he turned and looked at her through the wall of light, she was so certain. This was what Macy had been waiting for—the reason she had come here all those mornings and sat in the rain. Why she came alone. So she would be ready when Nick came back.

Chapter Nine

"Nick!" Macy called out again, this time on purpose. Her hood was making her feel claustrophobic so she threw it off, letting the water that dripped off the trees run down her face. The ghost just stood there, watching her through the Door. Macy started to slowly walk to that side of the Door, stepping gently on the brambles and soggy leaves. She felt like the ghost was a bird that would startle the moment she made a sound. *Nick, please*, she thought. Then she wondered what she would see. Would he look like he did in the hospital? Or would he look like himself?

When Macy first saw her brother after the

accident, she was so sure that it wasn't him. His face was red and puffy, with a bandage covering his missing eye. His forehead was lumpy and looked as shiny and purple as an eggplant—so swollen that Macy thought it might split open as she stood there, trying not to scream. *Not him not him not him.* Those were the words she kept saying over and over in her head. She could feel the words in her mouth—the muscles of her tongue trying, but failing, to say them aloud.

Now, as she took the few steps around the Door, all Macy could think was *Let it be Nick, let it be Nick.* She was so sure that when she saw his light brown hair—so like her own—and dark jeans, she almost threw her arms around the ghost. But when she wiped the rain out of her eyes with the back of her wrist—the knife still clasped firmly in her hand—she knew she was wrong. It wasn't Nick. It was just another strange ghost that she'd have to kill.

Macy pulled her hood back up and inspected

the ghost. He was very close to her brother's build—in between Dominick and Jackson's heights, but broader. His hair was shorter than Nick's and was actually quite a bit darker. Almost black. She didn't know why she had thought his hair was Nick's color. She had just seen what she wanted to see, she supposed.

She couldn't tell what color the ghosts' eyes were, but he was watching her. He tracked her movements as she took a final step and stood directly in front of him. The ghost wore jeans and a plaid button-up shirt with a few buttons open at the neck. He either looked very retro or had been dead for a few decades. It was hard to tell, since people were always wearing shabby-chic crap they found in thrift stores. There was something off about his clothes, however, and she soon realized what it was—he wasn't wearing a coat. But the rain fell straight through him, so he probably didn't mind.

It had only been about thirty seconds since the

ghost passed through the Door. In that time he had only stood there, as though waiting for Macy to make a move. His eyes asked her a question, but she didn't think she knew the answer yet. Not an answer she wanted. Macy took a step toward the ghost and held out her hand. *Stupid, stupid,* said the inner voice that sounded a bit like Claire. *So stupid.* Macy wanted to know how real he was—if he was just an echo. Also, it was easier for her to dispatch a ghost if she could lay her hands on him. With the hand not gripping her butterfly knife, Macy tried to touch the ghost's shoulder.

Her hand went right through the plaid fabric. Macy tried not to be disappointed, because that would make her a crazy person. She shouldn't be disappointed that the ghost she was trying to destroy was weak and couldn't touch her. Even though she knew the ghost wasn't Nick, those few moments when she had thought it might be her brother had shaken her. A small, tiny part of her thought that maybe—if this ghost wasn't just an echo—it might mean that her brother could still come back. That he might still know her. It was as dumb as thinking that if you stepped on a crack you'd actually break your mother's back.

Macy took a step back and prepared to dissolve this young man, just as she had the little boy who was sitting in the rain. It should have been easy, like flicking the rain off the brim of her hood. He was only an echo. Macy closed her eyes and felt her mind latching into him, feeling for the edges of him—the outline of his being. Sometimes this part felt strangely intimate, like she could feel the inside of the ghosts' heads, or like she was reaching her hand into their chests like that creepy fuck from *Indiana Jones and the Temple of Doom* who had pulled out a guy's beating heart.

This time, as she reached out towards the ghost, it felt different. Instead of just catching a firm hold of the wispy edges of the ghost, Macy felt like something was pushing back at her—a pulsing that filled her concentration like a steady, beating heart.

She opened her eyes. The ghost was still watching her and his hand was raised. "Wait," he said. His voice was soft, like leaves rustling down an empty road. "Just wait a minute."

Macy's first instinct was not to wait, but rather to plunge the knife into his neck. That's what smart girls did—girls who didn't end up murdered in a soggy, depressing patch of trees. But the ghost was just an echo. A shadow. He couldn't actually hurt her. So she did wait. While Macy stared at his throat, trying to decide what to do, she noticed that she could sort of see through the ghost. Earlier, when she was standing behind the Door, Macy had been able to see the ghost through the pulsing curtain of the Door. Now she could faintly see the Door throb and ripple behind him. What if more ghosts came out of the Door while she hesitated? What if there were too many and they swarmed her? Macy hadn't actually heard of ghosts working together. She didn't even know if one ghost could see another. How horrible if all of the ghosts that roamed the world thought they were the only ones. How lonely.

Macy knew she was stalling. She didn't want to kill this ghost, who was looking her in the eye and asking for mercy.

"Who are you?" she finally said.

He looked up, into the rain. Then he looked back at her. "I . . . I need to do something." He didn't answer her question. Had he even heard her? When the rain fell through the ghost he appeared to flicker, like the TV did when her mom vacuumed too close to it. The way he spoke to her, he didn't sound like an echo. Dominick had told her about stronger ghosts—ones who could carry on a conversation—but she had never met one. Even the man with the goggles, who was strong enough to burn down a building if he chose, hardly seemed to speak. But her hand had gone right through this boy. What was he?

"What's your name?" She tried again.

He blinked, as though trying to remember. Macy hoped that when she died she wouldn't come back. She didn't want to be a shadow. She didn't want to forget herself.

"Henry," he said at last. His voice was getting louder, more real sounding. "Henry Grey."

"Oh shit." Macy brushed the rain out of her face again, almost stabbing herself in the cheek. She put the knife back in her pocket, knowing she could get it back out and open in less than three seconds if she needed to. Jackson had timed her.

"Grey?"

He paused, raising one hand to his collarbone. Macy didn't know if he realized he was doing it. "I think . . . yes. That's my name. Henry Grey." He shook his head. "I'm really here? It feels so . . . foggy. I can see you, but it's like you're down a tunnel or something." He took a step closer. "Too far away. Do I know you?"

"No." Macy took a step back. Her heel hit a

rotting log and she almost tripped. "You're dead. You know that, right?"

He blinked, then rubbed his face. "I guess. I mean, yeah . . . I know. I died, and then I was . . . somewhere else. For a long time. I'm not sure where that was. I was waiting for something, you know? Like I had a test to take or I had a doctor's appointment. But I just kept waiting."

Stab him! her Claire-voice said. It also sounded a bit like Jackson. *This isn't a fucking meet-and-greet!*

"You have to hide," she heard herself say.

The ghost's eyes widened. "Why?" He let his hands fall to his sides. Macy couldn't see anything wrong with him. No bruises, no broken bones. His face was pale with dark eyebrows and a small, delicate nose. He would have been cute if he was alive. One of those brooding boys in movies who think really deep thoughts, and, like, pine for things.

Macy shook her head in reply, but she didn't

really know what she would do yet. She should just do it—get rid of him so she wouldn't have to think about it anymore. But he just didn't look dead. And he was talking to her.

"I have to do something," the ghost—Henry—continued. "I have to stop something. It's why I died—I remember pieces of it. I remember running. I remember there wasn't enough time and I needed to find something. There was something I had to do, and then I died. I think . . . I think it was terrible. I think I was afraid." He spoke in a rush, but also in a kind of matter-of-fact tone, like he was just reading from a list of things to do today.

"Do you remember how you died?" Macy asked. She shivered and folded her arms across her chest. She could feel her heart beating in her throat.

"No. I remember that I was alive . . . and then I wasn't. I just . . . I wasn't . . . anymore."

You burned to death fifty years ago, Macy almost said, but she held her tongue. What if ghosts really were like sleepwalkers? You weren't supposed to wake a sleepwalker, right? Maybe you weren't supposed to tell a ghost how he died. She remembered the story of Henry Grey, but when she first saw the ghost she hadn't connected him to the picture she'd seen at the school. Principal Grey standing next to his nephew, his arm around the young man. It was up in one of the glass cabinets in the school hallway, next to some old trophies. If they had both died as the building collapsed, then why did Henry look so perfect? Why didn't he look like how he died, like the little broken girl from the church? Like Dom's poor sister? Why wasn't he crushed or burned? Did that mean that Nick could be okay when he came back? Could he be normal?

Macy tried to think of a question to ask him—something that would help her decide what to do. Finally, she asked "What do you want?"

Henry flickered again, the light of the Door pulsing behind him. "I want . . . " He rubbed his face again, like he was exhausted. Could a ghost even feel his own skin? "I just want to remember. I just want time."

"You're not supposed to be here," Macy whispered.

"I know." He turned his green eyes to her. At least, she thought they were green. It was hard to tell in the shadows, and with the light of the Door behind him. "I . . . I think I used to be like you. I think I used to know what ghosts were. What I am. I'm a ghost." He frowned and looked down at his shoes. "How strange."

He looked back at Macy. "I just need to remember. It's important. I need to do something, then I'll go. I just need a little more time." Macy hadn't said that she was going to make him . . . *go away*. Kill him. She hadn't said those words. But he seemed to know. Though he said everything so calmly, Macy could hear the pleading in his voice. He was asking her permission. He was asking her for more time.

Time. Could Macy give him time? Was that something a person had the power to give? She thought about Nick, and how his birthday meant nothing now. He had no more time.

"Okay," Macy said. "Tomorrow. I'll come back tomorrow." Henry was just another echo, like the girl in the church or that woman in the movie theater. He was harmless. Henry couldn't even touch her. What could he do in one day?

"A day," Henry said, looking up to the tops of the trees. "It's been years, hasn't it? I didn't recognize it at first, but this is where the school was. It burned, didn't it?"

"Yes." Macy watched him, wondering how he'd react. He seemed so calm. "I'm sorry. You've been dead for . . . um . . . fifty years."

He nodded, like he'd expected her to say that. "These trees weren't here before. They're so tall."

Macy didn't know what to say. He reminded her of a movie she saw once, where coma patients wake up, and they don't recognize anything. Or

The Shawshank Redemption, where an old man got out of jail after decades and decades of being locked up and he didn't understand how the world worked anymore. She was pretty sure that character ended up killing himself.

"I'll be back tomorrow. Just . . . just stay here, okay?"

Henry nodded and began to drift among the trees, looking around. Macy could barely see his feet move—he just seemed to float, like a twig caught in a stream. When she walked away, he was still looking out toward where the trees thinned and you could see all the way to the water.

Chapter Ten

The next day Macy woke up at 4:30 a.m. She was quiet leaving the house. Hopefully she'd be back before her parents noticed she was gone. Her mom had thrown a fit yesterday. She had forgotten to text her mom after she left the funeral—and after Henry—well, Macy sort of forgot all about brunch. By the time she came home it was mid-afternoon and her mom was furious.

"It was disrespectful to me, and to your grandparents." Her mom had sat her down at the kitchen table and started boiling water for tea. "They came all this way to spend time with you, and then you just ditch us?"

Macy winced. When her mom said things like "ditch," it was like she was trying to sound younger than she was. Not that her mom was *that* old. But still, it sounded weird.

"I was just really upset after the—after Nick's thing, and I wanted to go see Claire. She's always there when I need to talk."

Macy didn't like to say *funeral* in front of her mom. It felt like she was saying lines from an after-school special about grief, but she thought her mom would buy it.

Her mom poured two mugs of peppermint tea. Macy's dad was in the other room watching football. He didn't like confrontation and hadn't really looked up from the TV when Macy walked in. She could hear her dad groan. The Seahawks must have fumbled the ball or something.

Her mom set a mug in front of Macy. "You're soaking wet. After you drink this you should go take a hot bath."

She could tell that her mom's anger was already

fading. Macy didn't usually do anything wrong, so being scolded was probably an equally bewildering experience for both of them.

"I'm sorry, Mom." Macy took a hesitant sip. It was still so hot that it burned the tip of her tongue. Her mom used to make her peppermint tea when she stayed home from school with a cold. The smell made her feel tiny, like she could fit in her mom's pocket. It wasn't a bad feeling.

"Why don't you take off your gloves? They must be soaked through." Her mom reached out for her daughter's hand. Macy jerked away, spilling scalding tea on her mom's hand. Her mom sucked in her breath and stood up, staring at Macy for an instant before turning and running her hand under the faucet.

"Jesus. Mom? You okay?" Macy set down her tea and stood behind her mom.

"Fine. Just a little burn." Her mom's voice wavered, just like it did at the church when she talked about the flowers.

Macy felt something inside her chest crumble. She hugged her mom around the waist. Her mom froze for a moment and then relaxed and patted Macy's arm with her dry hand. "I'll be fine. Finish your tea and I'll go up and run you a bath. Then we'll have an early dinner with Grandma and Grandpa. We can go out for Indian food—your favorite."

When her mom walked up the stairs and disappeared from sight, Macy had whispered, "Nick's favorite."

As Macy walked down the street at four thirty a.m., she was surprised to find that it wasn't raining. It was foggy though, and dark in that uncomfortable not-quite-night-but-not-quite-morning kind of way. Like the day didn't exist yet.

Macy was so tired that she felt like *she* didn't quite exist. The alarm on her phone (she had turned the volume way down and set it next to her head so her parents wouldn't hear) had woken her out of a deep sleep. She was so full of adrenaline from being jolted awake that her stomach was in a knot, and she had a sharp headache right between her eyes.

Macy should have called Jackson right away and told him about Henry. And she certainly should have told Dom. But she hadn't told anyone. She didn't know how.

It felt wrong to expose Henry when all he wanted was time to think—time to remember himself. But now Macy knew she had to take care of it. She had given him a day, or most of it, and she just couldn't let him stay any longer. She would handle this herself.

When Macy got to the Door, she didn't see Henry right away. Macy shined her flashlight around, and jumped when several little pairs of red eyes lit up in the distance. Probably deer or raccoons or something. There wasn't anything bigger than that in town, like a bear or a cougar. She hoped.

"Henry?" Macy whispered, her teeth beginning to chatter. Her raincoat wasn't very warm and she wished she had grabbed her down jacket, but that was still packed away in the garage with the other winter stuff.

She clenched her teeth together, looking around in the dark. Then she saw him. The ghost was sitting on a pile of broken bricks with his back to her.

"Henry." She said again, a little louder. He turned, and Macy was amazed that she could see him, even in the dark. His body was like the fog—gathering the first haze of morning light and making it brighter. He wore the same old, plaid shirt, and he had his arms wrapped around his knees.

"You're back? Is it tomorrow already?" His voice sounded brittle and far away.

Macy stepped over a fallen tree and walked

around the twisted remains of a merry-go-round. She sat on the bricks next to the boy. "Almost."

"But not quite?"

"No, I guess not. There's still some time before dawn." Macy looked where Henry was looking—out past the dark trees to the water that it was still too dark to see. She couldn't wait a few hours. There was school soon, and besides, did a few hours really matter? There was never enough time, ever. Nothing she did today would change that fact.

Henry reached out his hand and Macy flinched as it passed through her arm. "I'm not real, am I?" he said. Macy thought of Pinocchio—the little doll who wanted to be a real boy. She didn't know how to answer him.

"I remembered something yesterday, after you left. I remembered my car. It was brand new, and black. I washed it every day, and it smelled like . . . I can't remember. I can't really remember smells."

He held his legs closer. "Do you think someone else drove my car after I died?"

"I was supposed to get my brother's car when he graduated, but he crashed it." Macy didn't mean to say that. She had intended to close her eyes and pull the pieces of Henry apart until he vanished. "My brother died."

"It's not so bad."

"What?" Macy asked, startled.

"Being dead. It's not so bad. I bet he doesn't mind." Henry was looking at his own hand, twisting his wrist to inspect the back of his hand and then the palm. "I don't even mind this—not being able to touch things, I mean. It's just that I can't quite remember. I know it's important, but . . . it's like there are pieces missing. Parts of my mind are just . . . gone."

"Do you remember . . . " Macy paused, making sure she got the words just right. "Do you remember if there were others with you? When you were waiting on the other side of the Door? Were there other ghosts?"

"Like your brother?" Henry's voice was lower, with an edge she hadn't heard before. Like he was mocking her. But no, not quite mockery—more like he wanted her to know that he knew *exactly* what she was really asking. He wanted her to know that he had her figured out. It sent a shiver through her, deeper than the morning cold. Wasn't he just an echo?

"Yes," she said, trying to keep the desperation out of her own voice. "Did you see anyone else?"

"No. I was alone . . . wherever I was."

"But what's it like on the other side of the Door? How did you get out? Can you go back through?" She flung questions at him. It was getting lighter and time was running out. Soon she'd have to take care of him and leave.

Henry stood up. "Do you really want to know?" That edge was back in his voice.

She nodded. "Please. What's it like through the Door?"

He smiled a small, sad smile. "I'll tell you tomorrow."

Chapter Eleven

It had been two weeks since the lake and in that time, Jackson and Sam had begun a kind of . . . competition. No, that wasn't quite the right word. Maybe "conversation."

Sam started the whole thing when she sent him a link to a website about local ghost stories. "Pick one," she had texted. There were so many to choose from: a child who haunted an old hotel from the 1800s; the ghost of a woman who was supposed to have thrown herself from the lighthouse after she saw her husband's ship crash on the distant rocks; a dead sailor who wandered the docks at night.

Jackson chose the lighthouse.

Sam didn't think they needed to tell the others because the lighthouse ghost didn't have a reputation for killing anyone. Jackson was also pretty sure Sam was still getting shit from her brother about jumping into the lake.

But when they walked all the way out to the lighthouse—skipping last period so they would have plenty of time before it started to get dark—Jackson had to take Sam's word for it that there was no ghost. He probably wouldn't have been able to see the woman even if she had actually existed.

On the way back, Sam dispatched the ghost of an old lady whom Jackson couldn't see either. But it wasn't the right ghost. Jackson wanted the famous one—the tragic woman from the story. It was rather disappointing, but there were so many ghosts on Sam's list. There had to be another one that was real.

Jackson was also starting to wonder what the big deal was about the Door. If having a Door just meant was that there were a few extra ghosts wandering around, then why had crazy Lorna been so freaked out about it in the first place? Did she really have to murder a bunch of students in the 1960s to keep it closed?

It seemed like the payoff wasn't really that great, considering the cost. And Dom was finding out jack shit about closing the Door. He had mentioned a ritual in Arizona, where some guy had killed a few women, but there weren't any solid facts. And how did that actually help them close the Door, if there really was a ritual? Was Dom really going to start offing random people to close the Door? Somehow Jackson couldn't picture the little guy slitting people's throats. Sam, on the other hand . . .

When it was Sam's turn to choose from the list, she picked the child in the hotel. "What if it's like in *The Shining*," Sam had said, "and the kid's all like 'Red Rum, Red Rum!'"

They actually found a ghost that time. Sam and

Jackson walked into the hotel lobby one Saturday morning, and when there wasn't anyone at the front desk, they just started poking around the hotel by themselves.

Jackson was a little sorry he hadn't told Macy, because she would have loved the old building with its creaky hardwood floors. It smelled ancient—a kind of musty, peeling paint smell. But he liked hanging out with Sam without any of the others. Being with her was kind of like having a majestic bird—maybe a bald eagle—land on the hood of your car. You weren't going to fucking move.

When Sam found the boy in an upstairs bathroom, Jackson saw something, but it just looked like the old flower-print wallpaper was a little blurred by the sink. He would have thought it was just something in his eye if Sam hadn't knelt down and held out her hand.

"Hey, little guy," she said, with a voice that hardly sounded like Sam at all. It was so soft, and calm. Then she stood up abruptly, looking a little pale.

"Did you do it?" Jackson asked, squinting his eyes at the blurry spot. "Is he gone?"

Sam shook her head. "Nah. Let's just leave him. For now." Then she looked at Jackson, narrowing her eyes. "But don't tell the others, okay? They don't need to know about this."

Jackson nodded, but wondered why it mattered. It was just a little kid.

For Jackson's second choice, he went with the dead sailor. On a Tuesday night he and Sam walked down to the docks after the moon was high in the sky. It needed to be that night because legend had it that the sailor only came out after dark and only showed himself on clear nights. They had to go before it started raining again.

It was fucking freezing beneath the wide open sky. The stars felt like little shards of ice pressing down on his skin, and Jackson could see his breath. Somehow he had missed the beginning of fall. It was summer, and then suddenly it was full-blown fall-almost-winter with leaves piling up on the sidewalks and pumpkin spice lattes everywhere. Before he knew it, November would be back again, and then it would be a full year since his mom had died. He had heard the expression that time flies when you're having fun, but this year had been shitty, so that didn't explain why the months were zooming past.

When they got to the harbor they found that the ramp to the docks—which was high above the beach at low tide and almost flush with the water at high tide—was locked. "What the fuck?" Sam said, rattling the metal gate that blocked their way.

"We could climb it," Jackson suggested, though he wasn't actually sure that was a good idea. It had a row of those spikes on the top of the gate that were supposed to keep birds from perching on it. Could be pretty painful if they slipped. "Or we could swim around and climb on the dock from the water?"

Sam snorted. "I think I'm done with swimming for a while."

"Pick the lock?" Jackson wasn't serious about that one (or, to be honest, the swimming idea). The only time he had been in actual trouble—like, with the law—was when he and Macy tried to shoplift a jumbo-sized pack of M&M's in sixth grade. The bag had torn open under his coat and candy went everywhere. Macy pretended that she didn't even know him and had just walked out of the store.

Everyone thought Macy was Little Miss Perfect, but she was actually kind of a bitch sometimes.

Sam shined her flashlight at the lock. "Yeah, I could probably manage it."

Before Jackson could decide if he should tell Sam he was kidding—or just go with it as per his *agree-with-everything-Sam-said* plan—he saw something move beneath them. Someone was walking along the beach below.

It was low tide, so a wide expanse of

seaweed- and barnacle-covered rocks was exposed below the ramp. The ghost wore ripped jeans that hung loosely off his skinny body—so low that Jackson could see where his hips jutted out. He had a patchy beard and a heavy coat that looked like army surplus. He was holding a bottle of something and was swearing to himself.

"I can see him," Jackson whispered to Sam, feeling both stunned and a little proud. Maybe all his practice had paid off. "It's the sailor." The ghost didn't really look like a sailor, but Jackson was just so excited to actually see a ghost that he didn't stop to think about that part.

Sam stared open-mouthed at Jackson for a few seconds. Then she said in a low whisper, "You do realize that's just some dude, right? He's alive?"

"Sure—just joking. Ha, ha." But Jackson hadn't been joking. Not at all.

He was suddenly a bit relieved, for the first time, that he couldn't see ghosts. What if he couldn't tell the difference? What if he had walked up and stabbed this (homeless?) man in the neck with something like Macy's sharp little butterfly knife because he couldn't tell a real live person apart from a ghost?

Chapter Twelve

That's when they decided to just scrap it and go back to Sam's house. It was still early, only about nine p.m., and when they got to the house they found Trev and Dom at the kitchen table playing a drinking game. The object of the game was apparently to see how many shots Trev could drink, while Dom just watched Trev get wasted because he wasn't supposed to mix painkillers and alcohol. Trev was winning, according to Trev.

Jackson was just going to drop Sam off and head home, but then he noticed Macy sitting next to Dom. It didn't look like Macy had seen Jackson yet, and for a moment he felt like walking back out the front door. Then Sam took his hand and pulled him along with her into the kitchen. Sam took the shot glass out of her brother's hand and tipped it back. She coughed. "What's this shit?"

Trev held up a bottle of peach schnapps. "Macy brought it, 's terrible," Trev slurred.

Macy grinned her *I'm-pretending-to-enjoy-myself* grin. "I found it in Nick's room," she said.

Jackson could always tell when Macy fake-smiled because she held her eyes open too wide and looked a little crazy. Ever since her brother's funeral Macy had been acting really weird. And not just the regular "seeing ghosts" kind of weird—a whole new level of moody shit. Whenever Jackson tried to talk to Macy, it felt like only part of her was in the room. He wondered if it had anything to do with Dom. Were they actually "doing it like rabbits," like Trev had said earlier?

As far as Jackson knew, Macy hadn't *done it* with anybody yet. But then, Macy didn't know about the girl Jackson had sex with when his parents sent him to summer camp after ninth grade. Courtney, with long black hair. She showed him how to put on a condom and they did it in the empty cabin that everyone said the counselors were using to hook up. He never told Macy about Courtney. Maybe he would have told her if she was a guy. But he could just picture the way Macy would have fake-smiled while pretending not to be hurt. And then she would have looked at Jackson differently. But he hadn't felt any different. He was still himself.

Jackson sat down next to Sam, grabbed the bottle, and took a long swig. The sweet liquid burned on the way down. "What was Nick doing with this shit?"

Macy apparently wasn't drinking the peach stuff, but she did have a beer. "I think it was for one of his girlfriends. He probably kept it around for when she came over, and they, you know." She wrinkled her nose and took a sip of her beer.

Jackson took another long gulp of the schnapps, then passed it to Sam.

"Hell no," she said, passing it along to her brother, who poured himself another shot.

"Actually, changed my mind, 's good." Trev's head drifted lower to the table as he lifted his hand, so his lips met the shot glass somewhere in the middle.

"So," Jackson started, as though it was a natural transition, "Dom. Did you find out anything today? Any closer to getting that Door closed?" The bottle came back to Jackson, so he took another long drink. Trev was right. After the first few drinks the peach started to taste kinda good—sort of like a peach cobbler.

"No, man. Nothin' today." Dom rubbed his eyes, like it was such a huge effort just to sit there, talking. What a prick.

"What about the 'ritual'? Anything going on with that?" Jackson asked.

Dom looked over at Macy, then back to

Jackson. "No. Nothing new. Well, I did find another possible case, but it was really old. From the 1950s. Another set of four murders, right next to a Door."

"Wait . . . how do you know about Doors from the 1950s? Didn't you just start researching this stuff a few years ago?"

Sam put her hand on Jackson's arm and handed him the bottle again. It was almost empty. "Jackson," she said. "You don't think we, like, discovered the Doors, do you?"

Jackson thought about it for a second. He actually didn't know anything about what the three of them did or didn't do before they got to Grey Hills. "Of course not," he said. "Because . . . " He took another sip. It started to taste bad again—like Jolly Ranchers. "Well," he continued after he swallowed, "Lorna knew about Doors, so others must have already known about them. Unless you're also time travelers."

Macy perked up. "That'd be an awesome movie, right?"

Jackson nodded, "Totally!" For just a second, it felt like the start of one of their old conversations where they just talked about movie shit—both actual movies and movies that should have been made. Back when Macy actually used to talk to him. Then her face seemed to close up again and she took another sip of her beer.

"You know," Jackson began, "I don't really get what's so bad about the Door. I mean, what's really happened since it opened? Like, a few ghosts wander around town, just haunting up the place? They don't seem to really be doing anything that bad."

Macy started to scrape at the label on her bottle with a fingernail. Jackson tried to meet her eye, but she didn't look up from the beer.

Then Trev piped up. "Hey sis, we should just tell them, right?"

Sam frowned. "You need a glass of water, bro. And then you need to lie down."

Trev shook his head. "Nope. We should just tell them." He turned to Macy. "Sam doesn't want people to know what happened. But she doesn't get to make the plans anymore. I get to make the plans because she jumps in lakes and smells like duck shit. So I get to decide."

Trev wasn't really making sense anymore. Jackson wondered how full the bottle was when Macy brought it over. Pretty damn full, based on Trev's wobbly head and watery eyes. And who knows what he had been drinking before she got there.

"Okay . . . " Macy said, leaning slightly away from Trev as he swayed in his seat.

"Dom, you wanna do something here?" Sam said, scooting her chair out like she was going to stand up. But she didn't. She just held the bottle tighter. Dom shrugged, then placed a hand over his hurt shoulder. Like he had to keep reminding them that he was the one who was shot.

Trev continued. "You know where we got all of this from? Maps and shit? Our dad. And you know where he is now?" Then he stopped talking and waited for them to answer.

"Um . . . dead?" Jackson finally said. "And that's why you can see ghosts? Like the rest of us?"

Trev shook his head in wide, sluggish motions. "Wrong! Dad's not dead. Dad's," he did a little flourish with the shot glass, "in jail."

"Stop it," Sam said. The blood had drained from her already pale face, and her hands were shaking. "Just stop it." She looked almost as bad as when Trev fished her out of the lake.

"You know our dad killed our mom? And our little brother? That he beat them to death with his bare hands? Yeah. That's what they told us, anyway. That's what the papers said. That he killed her and our brother. They said he 'snapped.'" Trev tried to make air quotes, but just managed to drop the mostly empty shot glass he was still holding. "But it wasn't him. That's the part they won't tell us. It wasn't our dad. A ghost got inside him. That's what went wrong with his head, 's why he did it. A fucking ghost burrowed its way into Dad's brain."

Sam looked like she was going to be sick. Jackson wasn't sure if he was seeing grief flash across her face or if she was just really, really angry. "Stop. Now," she said again.

But Trev kept talking. "Dad worked for people who studied the Doors. When . . . when it happened and Dad went to jail, those people gave us fifteen million dollars. Who gives that kinda money to orphans? I'll tell you—guilty people."

"It was a life insurance policy," Sam said quietly. "You know that. And we're not orphans. Dad's still alive."

Trev shook his head again. "I *don't* know that. They told us that, but I *don't* fucking know that. All I know is that a ghost got inside his head.

That's what they do. If they don't drown you or burn you to death, they'll fucking crack open your brain and climb in."

No one else was looking at Macy—Dom and Sam were both just staring at Trev—but Jackson saw her open her mouth a few times, like she wanted to ask something. Finally, she said, "Can any ghost do that? Get inside a person?"

"No—" Dom started to say, but Trev cut him off.

"You don't fucking know that, Dominick Vega. How could you know that? I taught you all this and now *you're* the expert?"

Dom didn't answer, and Trev didn't say anything else. He just grabbed the almost empty bottle of schnapps out of his sister's hand and stomped up the stairs.

When no one spoke, Jackson tried to fill the awkward silence. "Well, that was . . . "

"Don't," Sam said. "It wasn't anything. Just . . . let's just drop it."

Macy didn't look like she wanted to drop it, but she kept her mouth closed. Then, when Sam retrieved a bottle of whiskey from a kitchen cupboard, Macy stood up. "I'm gonna take off."

Jackson knew he should offer to walk Macy home, but Sam looked so breakable—like her skin was a windshield that had fractured, but was still clinging together in one shattered sheet. If Sam did break apart, Jackson wanted to see what was inside.

Chapter Thirteen

Claire wanted to go to the mall and look for a Halloween costume and then see a new movie about a possessed china doll. Macy wanted to escape her life for a few hours, so she climbed into the passenger seat of her friend's Golf, turned up the music, and put her feet up on the dashboard.

Almost three weeks had gone by and Macy still hadn't said a word about Henry to anyone. She could feel the lie in the back of her mouth like a sore throat. Her stomach hurt a lot lately, and the Tums she constantly chewed didn't do anything except make her breath smell like medicine.

Macy didn't know why she was so certain that

she couldn't tell the others about Henry. But she felt like telling them would be something she could never take back—not ever. Macy was sure they would kill him and whatever he was trying to remember would be lost forever.

She chewed another Tums—cherry flavored—and rolled down her window because the car felt too small.

"I was thinking of being a sexy pirate. You know, 'shiver me timbers' or 'I'll walk *your* plank,'" Claire said in a seductive purr that she totally pulled off.

"Slutty eyepatch? Sexy pegleg?" Macy laughed. It had finally stopped raining a few days earlier. The fall colors weren't very bright this year—more faded oranges and browns than reds—but the trees still looked a bit startling against the blue sky.

Claire laughed. "A pegleg *is* basically a portable stripper pole. What about you? What are you going to be?"

Macy hadn't actually thought about Halloween

yet. Claire still made a huge deal about it, but ever since she got too big to trick-or-treat Macy had thought Halloween was kind of lame. Everyone just dressed up as sexy versions of boring things. Sexy cat. Sexy witch. Sexy princess.

Last year Macy had dressed as a zombie, which was really hard to make slutty. She wore her regular jeans and t-shirt, and painted her mouth so it looked like her lower jaw was rotting off. She carried around a plastic container of pink Jell-O that was molded to look like brains. Claire was Tinkerbell, complete with sexy green fishnet stockings. It was her little sister's costume from the year before—except for the fishnets. Those were all Claire's.

"So, you and Dom?" Claire asked, not looking away from the road. "Anything happen yet?"

Macy shook her head. "Not really. I don't know . . ."

Claire popped her gum loudly—a trick Macy had envied when she first met her friend in seventh grade and still wasn't able to do. She always ended up swallowing the gum. "You don't know *what*? You don't know if he likes you? Duh."

Macy chewed another Tums. Some kind of green flavor this time—mint? Apple? "It's complicated."

"Is that what your Facebook status says?"

"Ew! No."

"Mace . . . nothing is complicated unless you make it complicated. Be fearless. Kiss him." Claire started singing the *sha-la-la-la* part of the "Kiss the Girl" song from *The Little Mermaid*.

"Ugh. Don't ever do that again." Macy didn't tell Claire about the morning after Nick's funeral, when she *had* kissed Dom. Sort of. He hadn't mentioned his sister again since that day, or the kiss.

He probably didn't know it had happened, because Macy was a creepy stalker who only kissed boys when they were asleep. She sometimes wondered if that conversation had even happened, or if she had made it all up in her head. Some kind of grief hallucination or something.

Claire sped up and the glove compartment started to rattle. The Golf didn't like high speeds. "Just don't be afraid to take a chance, okay?" Claire's voice was unusually serious. "You deserve something nice."

It took about forty-five minutes to drive to the mall (forty with Claire driving). When they finally pulled into the parking lot Macy started looking through her purse for a coupon—two for one pretzels—so she didn't see the woman until they were about to hit her. Macy screamed. Claire slammed on the brakes, but it was too late. They ran right over her. Macy saw the woman's eyes widen, and her blond hair flew back as they slammed into her.

"What. The. Fuck." Claire was gripping the steering with both hands. She was shaking. "What happened?"

"You didn't see her?" Macy pulled open her

door and tried to run outside to find the woman, but was jerked back. She had forgotten to take off her seatbelt. As she fumbled with her seatbelt, a few cars honked and drove around them.

Claire's eyes were huge. "I hit someone?"

Macy climbed out, and looked at the front wheels—bracing herself for what she thought she'd see. But there was nothing. Just wheels. Fucking ghosts. Again.

Claire had her phone out—probably about to call 911—but Macy waved her arms, shaking her head. "Sorry! There's no one here!"

Claire rolled down the window. "So . . . I didn't hit someone?"

"No . . . I guess I was seeing things." Macy stared at the tires. There was no way she was ever going to get used to seeing ghosts. No fucking way.

Claire pulled forward into a parking space, then stopped the car again. She got out—her feet unsteady on her two-inch wedges. Then she walked over to Macy and punched her in the arm.

Claire hadn't done that since eighth grade, when it was cool to give each other "dead arms" in the hall.

"I swear to God! Never do that to me again. I almost swallowed my fucking tongue!"

Macy rubbed her arm. Claire had hit her pretty hard and her arm was tingling. "Sorry!"

"Next time you scream like that, someone had better be dying." Claire stalked off toward the mall entrance, not waiting to see if Macy was following. Her friend would calm down in a few minutes, Macy knew, and then she'd want to go straight to the food court for a pretzel and a smoothie.

Ever since the gym fire, Claire had kind of a short fuse. It was easy for Macy to forget that while she had been trying to stop the ghost with the goggles from killing everyone, Claire was scared out of her mind in the girl's locker room with no idea what was happening.

She'd told Macy about it after Macy told her the Dom-approved version of things—that Macy and the others had run outside and waited behind the school for the fire trucks. Before the fire started, Claire had gone to the locker room to clean the paint out of her hair. She was bent over the sink, her hair unbraided and loose under the faucet, when she heard the screams. At first she thought the senior prank was starting up again. But then she smelled smoke and the screams got louder and louder.

Claire thought of all those school shootings and terrorist attacks, and she ran into a bathroom stall and locked the door. She got out her phone and started to call 911, but then dropped her phone in the toilet because her hands were shaking so much. She fished out her phone and crouched with her feet up on the toilet because she thought that maybe someone wouldn't look for her there. She tried to call 911 again, with her toilet-water soaked phone pressed to her ear, but it didn't work.

Then she waited. And waited, breathing in and out so quietly that her head began to swim.

She waited while she heard the sirens and waited when she heard the faint sound of a gunshot from outside the school. Claire waited until a fireman came in and carried her out. Claire fainted when she saw him. She would be forever mortified, she told Macy, that a hot fireman had to rescue her from a toilet.

Claire still didn't know that it was Dom who got shot that night. No one knew that part. Trev and Sam drove him to a hospital in another town. Sometimes Macy thought she should just tell Claire about the ghosts, but she didn't know how her friend could ever believe her. And it was nice, once in a while, to just hang out with Claire and not be a part of that world.

After they ate their pretzels and drank their smoothies—Macy's treat—Claire steered Macy towards one of those costume shops that pop up in malls around Halloween before they turn into Christmas boutiques.

"Come on, we're going to find you the perfect costume." Claire was her normal self again, only a thousand times more "Claire" because she was on a mission. "Something pretty this time. No zombies!"

"What about prom queen zombie?"

"Maybe . . . only if you show a lot of leg. Or tasteful side-boob." Claire flipped through a rack of dresses until she found an indecently short pirate costume. "Perfecto! Now to find you something."

When Claire had her mind set on something, she was kind of like the second Terminator—the one who could morph into different shapes and sometimes looked like a puddle of silver ooze. That guy just kept coming, even if he was being shot or hit by a car. That's exactly what Claire was like when she was shopping—except for the oozing part. She would probably punch Macy in the arm a second time if she ever heard her describe Claire as "oozing."

"What about this?" Claire held up a very short black dress that was only identifiable as a witch costume and not just a regular short black dress by the pointy hat.

"Lame."

"This?" Claire showed Macy a Cleopatra costume that was basically a bikini and a rubber snake. "I could do your makeup. You'd blow Dom out of the water."

"Not a chance. But that reminds me, I thought of another slogan for your pirate costume: 'Thar she blows!'"

Claire stuck out her tongue. She didn't give up, even after Macy systematically rejected a sexy Raggedy Ann, sexy Pocahontas, and a strangely modest clown costume, complete with huge floppy shoes.

"I'm not wearing any of these. Disgusting." Macy wrinkled her nose.

"You have to choose something. You can't come to my party in jeans." Claire had moved on to the accessories section and was hoisting a fake cutlass for her pirate costume.

"You're having a party?" Something red caught Macy's eye. It was a long, red cape with a hood. She couldn't really feel the material with her gloves on, but it looked soft and shiny.

"Well . . . I'm planning this thing with Trev. It was his idea—a big party at his house. I figured he told you, 'cause you're always over there." Macy knew that Claire was a little hurt by all the time she spent with the others without inviting her. But Macy just didn't have the energy to think about Claire's feelings all the time.

"Nope. He didn't mention it." Macy picked up the cape and tried it on. It was probably supposed to be part of a Little Red Riding Hood costume. Wrapping the silky material around her shoulders, she noticed that there were pockets on the inside of the cape. Perfect.

Claire smiled. "Well, we're only going to invite other juniors—no fucking seniors." Claire said that last part a little too loud, and a child who was trying on a set of vampire fangs looked up. The kid's mother frowned at Claire and pulled her son towards the other side of the store. The little boy took the fangs out of his mouth and set them back on the shelf. Nasty.

"So, you and Trev are planning this? Anything going on there?" Macy raised her eyebrows.

"Um . . . you do know he's gay, right?"

Macy did *not* know that. Her face flushed, so she turned away and pretended to be looking at the tag on the cape. "Sure. Just joking."

There was so much that Macy didn't actually know about her new . . . was "friends" even the right word? She thought about what Trev had told them about his dad. Was that even true? Sam, who usually acted like some bipolar anime character, had looked like her brother had just punched her in the stomach.

"So, what are you gonna be?" Claire asked, pointing to the red cape Macy was still holding.

Macy put the cape back on and spun around. "Fearless."

Chapter Fourteen

When Macy checked her phone after the movie she had twenty-three missed calls, all from her parents. She didn't even bother listening to the messages, but just called home.

"Where are you?" Her mom sounded pissed. Again. Macy tried to think what she could have possibly done wrong this time. Of course there were plenty of things her mom could be pissed about—like Macy hanging out with a boy in his bedroom, or sneaking out of the house before dawn to talk to a ghost. But her mom didn't know about any of those things. Had Macy let Jasper outside by mistake? Did she break something? What the fuck?

Macy tried to keep her voice calm and happy. Normal teenage girl voice. "I'm at the mall with Claire. Remember? We just saw a movie?"

"Claire's with you? Thank god. Tell her to call her mother this instant. I mean it, right now. I'll wait." Macy pulled the phone away from her face. She had been holding it so tightly against her head that her ear hurt.

"Claire, it's my mom. She said you have to call your mom." Claire shrugged and took out her lip gloss.

Macy put the phone back to her ear. Her mom spoke before Macy could even say she was back, like she had psychic mom powers. "Macy, why hasn't Claire called yet? Is she really with you?"

Macy almost said "What the fuck?" out loud, but managed to bite it back. *Normal, happy teenage voice.* "She's about to call. Besides, how do you know she hasn't?"

"Because her mom is sitting next to me."

Macy's face flushed, and then felt icy—like she had a fever. "What happened?" The last time her mom was so weird was when she told Macy that Nick was in an accident. Macy could barely speak when she asked "Is it Jackson?"

"No, honey. Jackson's fine. He answered his phone right away, unlike some people. It's someone else. They won't tell us who."

"Who what? Someone's dead?"

"Just come home. We'll talk about it when you get here. Don't let Claire speed."

"She doesn't speed."

"Just tell her to drive safely."

Once Macy's mom finally hung up, Macy turned to her friend. Claire's face looked stricken.

"What happened?" Macy still had no idea what her mom was talking about.

But Claire was still talking to her mom. "In the harbor? Really? Okay, I'll be home soon. No,

I won't speed. Jesus, Mom, I just said I wouldn't fucking speed. Okay. Love you too."

Claire dropped her phone back in her purse and turned to Macy. "The police found someone's body in the harbor. They haven't released the age or gender, so of course our parents assumed we were dead. Did they think 'we'll be at the mall' meant we were going skinny dipping in the cold-ass water?"

"Is that what happened?"

"What?" Claire fiddled with her phone, turning the screen on and off.

"Someone was skinny dipping?"

"I don't know. Jesus . . . is this shit ever going to end?"

Macy remembered saying something very similar to Dom, right after Nick's funeral. It was sometimes too easy to forget that, even without ghosts, life could be pretty fucking terrible.

"They don't know who it was?" Macy asked.

"No, not yet. What if it's someone from school?"

Three days later a jogger found a second body below the bluffs. He almost didn't notice the woman's twisted form where it lay among the driftwood and other beach rubble that collected at the high water line. It was her hair that caught his attention—it was purple.

She was all cut up and had a broken neck. The police ruled it a likely suicide. They decided that the gash on her neck was from a tree branch when she hit the ground.

Macy saw the woman's ghost as she walked to Dom's house after school. The ghost was standing beside the twin's yellow house, looking out over the bluff. At first, the woman's bright purple hair distracted Macy from the blood running down her arm and dripping onto the ground, so she didn't even realize right away that she was a ghost. Macy actually thought how peaceful the woman seemed looking out over the water. But then the woman turned and Macy saw the glistening red of her neck and how her blood soaked the front of her dress.

Macy was so startled she cried out "No!" holding her hand out between her and the bloody woman. The ghost stopped and looked down at her ruined shirt. She put a hand up to her neck and pulled it away covered in blood. The woman's face crumpled and she shook her head.

No, she mouthed, but Macy couldn't hear anything. The woman's purple hair started to fade to a pale lavender and then just a smoky gray. The red of her blood faded too. As she began to disappear, the ghost put her hand back to her neck and held it there. She kind of rocked back and forth on her heels.

"Wait," Macy whispered. The woman just looked so surprised by it all. Macy wished that the woman could have just a few more minutes. Just a little more time.

Macy pressed her hand to her own neck, feeling her pulse strong against her fingertips. It took six heartbeats for the woman to fade completely away. Macy held her breath the whole time.

"I don't think it was a suicide," Macy said. She had gathered everyone around the kitchen table, including Jackson, who had to walk there from his house. By that time, they had read online about the woman's body on the beach—that it was a suspected suicide.

"I saw her," Macy explained. "Her ghost, I mean. She had a cut on her neck, but she didn't look like she fell off a cliff. Wouldn't she have broken legs? More cuts? But it was just her neck."

"So you think someone killed her and made it look like a suicide?" Trev asked, not even trying to turn this into a joke. Trev being completely serious was kind of freaky. Ever since he told them about his dad, he had been acting like nothing happened—just joking around like usual—until now. Macy liked him better when he was joking. He was kind of like the canary in the coal mine. As long as he was joking, things couldn't be all that bad.

"But is that really how it works? Do ghosts always come back looking like how they died?" Macy thought about Henry. He looked so— perfect. He didn't look burned or broken. He just looked like a teenage boy. But Macy definitely couldn't use Henry as an example. His existence felt like an oven she had forgotten to turn off. She couldn't help thinking about him all the time.

Every time Macy saw Dom she almost told him about Henry. But something always stopped her. She didn't want to make a mistake that could cost Henry his . . . life? Macy just wanted to be completely sure before she did something she couldn't take back. And every day Henry was remembering more and more. He was bound to remember what he was supposed to be doing— what was so important that he'd crossed through the Door.

Sam nodded. "I think so. That's how they've always looked to me." Sam chewed on the edge of her thumbnail. "If you're right about this, then that makes two people with cut throats. Dom, do you think it's really a pattern?"

Dom had been staring off into space. Macy wasn't even sure if he was listening, but then he said, "The other one . . . he had a cut throat too?"

"Among other things. He looked like he swam right into a boat propeller. That's actually what the police think."

"No one saw his ghost?"

"No," Macy said. "I don't think any of us were around when it happened. He must have faded away too quickly."

Jackson spoke up. "Who else could possibly

know about this ritual? Aren't we the only ones who know about this stuff?" He seemed to look pointedly at Dom.

Macy scowled at Jackson. She was starting to regret that Jackson knew about any of this. First he almost got Sam killed with his stupid ghost hunt, and it constantly felt like she needed to babysit him. Jackson couldn't even see ghosts and now he was practically accusing Dom of killing people.

At least that's how it sounded to her.

She hoped that the others didn't know what Jackson was hinting at, the way Macy could clearly see the thoughts churning behind Jackson's eyes. And Macy was sure that Jackson didn't even really think that—he was just always picking on Dom. Was Jackson jealous? Was that why he seemed to hate Dom? Well, he had fuck-all to be jealous about. Nothing had even happened between her and Dom. Not really.

Sam, who had stopped biting her nail and was now digging through a bowl of pretzels, answered

Jackson's question. "We have no idea who could know about a ritual. Lorna might not have been the only one in Grey Hills who knew something about the Doors, and we can't exactly ask her, can we?" Macy remembered Lorna's face as the ghost with the goggles wrapped his fiery arms around her. She still didn't know if Lorna had been pulled through the Door or if she had just burned up completely. What if she was still alive somewhere—beyond the Door? What if she was trapped there?

"Okay," Macy said. "Then what do we do? If it is a ritual, I mean? How do we stop whoever is killing people? How can we even find them?"

"Well," Dom started, tapping his finger on the table. "I mean . . . do we stop them?"

Trev narrowed his eyes. "What *exactly* do you mean?"

"Just, what if this *is* the ritual? What if it works? Do we have any other ideas for closing the Door? I've been looking for weeks and I've got nothing."

"No fucking way!" Trev knocked over the bowl

of pretzels with the swipe of his hand. It went sailing off the table and pretzels scattered all over the floor. The bowl was just plastic, so it bounced, but it was still pretty surprising. Macy was so startled that she started to hiccup.

Sam, who still had a handful of pretzels, threw one at her brother's head. "Fucking dramatic!"

"Fine," Dom said. "So we go to the police and tell them that someone is murdering people. They ask us how we know. We tell them that we think there might be a ritual that will close the Door to the Dead. They tell us to get the fuck out and stop wasting their time, or they actually detain us and suspect that *we're* some psychos who've been killing people. Is that your plan?"

"I don't know," Trev said. He ran his hand through his hair so it stuck up even more than usual. "But to actually root for this person to keep killing? It seems pretty fucked up."

"I'm not saying we help this person. But . . . do we even have a choice? And it's probably just a few really bizarre accidents, anyway. It happens. People doing stupid things all the time. People kill themselves."

Macy shook her head. "That woman didn't kill herself. She looked so surprised. And her neck. I don't believe it."

"Okay," Dom continued, "so there might have been a completely unrelated murder and a crazy boating accident. All I'm saying is that we don't really have a choice here. There's nothing we can do anyway. But if someone ends up closing the Door, is that so bad?"

"I can't even talk to you right now," Trev said. "You sound like a fucking Vulcan."

"You mean I'm being logical? I'm making too much sense?"

"It *is* kind of fucked up," Sam said. "Aren't we supposed to be saving people?" She popped a pretzel into her mouth and her crunching sounded extra loud because no one was talking. Macy kind of agreed with Sam and Trev, but she knew exactly what Dom meant. She wanted to show him that she understood. Macy tried to meet his eyes from across the table, but he wasn't looking at her. He was staring through the sliding glass doors again, out to the water. It reminded her of Henry, which made her feel dizzy—like she couldn't hold both guys in her head at the same time.

Since Nick's funeral, Macy had been back to see Henry almost every day. By the end of the first week he had remembered his parents and his house and what classes he was taking when he died. By the second week the sense that he had to do something—stop something—had grown stronger and stronger. He often just watched the Door. "There's something in there," he had told Macy, when she saw him that morning before school. "Something that wants out."

Macy knew they were supposed to want the Door to close, and she did—mostly. But a part of her still thought that, as long as it was open, her brother might come through. "What is it?" Macy had asked Henry. "What wants out?"

"I can't remember." He had put both hands in his hair and stayed that way, staring into the Door. He was still watching the Door when she walked away.

Chapter Fifteen

Jackson didn't mean to follow Macy when she left the yellow house that evening. He was going to catch up and walk with her until she got home. Keep her safe in case there really was some crazy killer on the loose. But right away she turned down the wrong street, and Jackson wanted to see what she was up to.

If she hadn't been so damn secretive in the past few weeks he wouldn't have done it. But if Macy was going to act like a fucking secret agent, then he was going to find out why.

The Door didn't even cross Jackson's mind until he realized Macy was heading for the school.

Sure enough, she went right past the entrance to the school and walked toward the path through the woods that would lead to the Door.

The whole time Jackson had stayed really far back—just close enough to see what streets she turned down. But now that he knew where she was headed, he figured he could beat her there and find a hiding spot. It was quicker to cut through the school. Macy was too short, but Jackson had no problem boosting himself over the chain link fence.

He tried to move quietly through the woods, but he kept stepping on shit like sticks and pop cans students always chucked over the fence. Littering fucks. Jackson had almost been enjoying himself earlier when he was following Macy. He was more than a little drunk off the whiskey that Sam had kept pouring, and he felt like a spy. But here, surrounded by trees and pieces of the dead school, Jackson was starting to get pretty pissed at Macy.

Why did she have to make everything so fucking difficult? What the hell was she thinking, wandering around at night? Macy was lucky he decided to follow her.

Jackson was right—he beat her to the Door. He couldn't really see the Door very well. It just appeared to be a sort of faint light that vanished when he looked at it straight on. But he could feel it.

The hair on his arms and on the back of his neck stood on end. It felt like someone was squeezing his heart in an unnatural rhythm.

Jackson hid behind a tree a few yards from the Door and tried to catch his breath. The whole thing made him a bit panicky—like he should run and keep running until there were miles between him and the Door.

He heard Macy before he saw her.

"Hello?" she whispered.

For an instant Jackson thought she was talking to him, and he felt silly and almost came out from behind the tree. But then she kept talking. "I know. But you're one to talk."

Jackson realized she wasn't talking to him. She was talking to someone he couldn't hear. He held his breath and peered around the tree, trying not to make a sound.

In the darkness he could see Macy standing next to the faint glimmer of the Door. He could just make out her face and the lines of her body. But he couldn't see anyone else with her.

Macy sat down, wrapping her arms around her knees like she did when she was feeling uncomfortable. But her voice didn't sound nervous. She laughed at something and shook her head, her ponytail swaying behind her.

Jackson wasn't stupid. At this point, it was obvious that Macy was talking to a ghost.

He closed his eyes, willing them to just *work better*. It wasn't fair that Macy could see ghosts and he couldn't. Was there some hierarchy that determined how good you were at seeing ghosts?

Was Macy's loss of her brother somehow worth *more* than Jackson's mom? That was bullshit. He couldn't imagine anything hurting worse—not even a brother dying.

When Jackson had confronted Macy in the girl's bathroom on the first day of school, she had told him that he couldn't understand. Like, just because he didn't have a brother, he couldn't possibly imagine how it felt when Macy lost hers? But he did. He fucking did.

Losing his mother was like losing a leg you didn't even know was holding you up and helping you walk. Like someone came by and just chopped it off and you had to keep hobbling along while you bled.

He knew exactly how Macy felt.

Jackson might not have a brother or sister, but he had Macy. Besides his parents, she was the only person in the world who felt like his own blood.

Not that she was like his sister. Otherwise it

would have been pretty fucking gross every time he had imagined her naked over the years.

Not that he necessarily wanted her to be naked. With him. He didn't know *what* he wanted from her.

Right now, he just wanted her back.

Kissing her had been a huge mistake. Big fucking disaster. It just seemed like what you're supposed to do when a girl you love is sitting next to you on the couch, already sharing your spit in the beer you've been passing back and forth.

He thought it might change things and he might feel something that wasn't either a scraped-clean emptiness or the too-full anger that sometimes came over him and made his eyes water.

Somehow he thought that he could love Macy in that other way, too. And kissing her would make him a different person. He couldn't be the person he was before his mother died and he didn't want to be the person he was after—pathetic and crumbling.

Jackson wanted to be something new. But kissing Macy was like the fucking Hindenburg. It just blew up his life in an entirely new way.

Chapter Sixteen

Almost an hour passed before Macy got up again. It was just past midnight and Jackson wondered if his dad would be angry that he wasn't home already. Sometimes his dad didn't even seem to notice when he came and went—like they were just roommates instead father and son. Other times his dad would overreact if Jackson was out past the nebulous curfew that his dad sometimes imposed. But, if tonight was like most school nights, his dad would already be asleep when he got back.

Jackson waited until Macy left before getting up from his hiding spot. He stood and faced the Door. "Nick?" he called out. "Is that you?" There was no answer, of course, and as hard as Jackson squinted, he couldn't see anything other than the faint, wavy glow.

Jackson hopped the fence and ran towards Macy's house. He knew just where to cut her off. She rounded a corner and he was already waiting, his arms crossed over his chest. "What the hell are you doing?" His voice came out a little harsher than he intended and he winced when she scowled at him.

"None of your fucking business." She was so tiny—almost a foot shorter than him. He often forgot that because she felt like such an extension of himself. Or used to, before he kissed her and fucked up everything between them. He thought they were back to normal after everything that happened the night of the Lock-In, but she just kept closing herself off. It was like she was always pissed off at him and it just made him pissed off in return.

"I know it's Nick." Jackson was so sure that

it felt like he knew. He could just picture Macy whispering with her brother in the dark. Plus, it was the only thing that made any sense. It had to be Nick. Why else would she be keeping this a secret? "Why didn't you tell me?" Jackson tried to make his voice less *judgey*, but it just came out a little flat. "You could have told me."

She closed the distance between them. "You followed me? Like some stalker?" Beneath the street lamp, Macy looked a little like a ghost her-self—or what he imagined a ghost would look like if he could see one clearly. She had her hood up so her face was shadowed, and her hands were shoved deep in the pockets of her coat.

"And you've been creeping around in the dark like a fucking idiot." Jackson tried to keep his voice low, but it came out as a hiss. "You could have been killed, you know that? Who just wan-ders around at night in a town full of ghosts? And now there might be a killer out here?" Jackson didn't think Macy had ever kept a secret from him before. It surprised Jackson how much it hurt—like he didn't even know her anymore. It was as if the old Macy—his Macy—had cracked open like one of those Russian dolls and a new Macy had stepped out. A dumber Macy.

Macy shook her head as if she couldn't believe what he was saying. "Do you have any idea how many ghosts I've killed walking by myself during the day? And it's not like they're asleep just because the sun's out. Do you think they're vampires?"

She hadn't even mentioned Nick. Did Macy think Jackson would just forget who she was seeing because she didn't mention his name? "It was Nick, wasn't it?" He put his hands out, palms up. "I totally get it. He's your brother—you don't want the others to do anything to him. But you could have told me." He closed his eyes, trying to get his voice under control. "Just—you can tell me. You can talk to me, you know? I'm here."

Macy shook her head again. But then she looked him in the eye. "If you tell the others, I'll never forgive you. Not ever. Understand? You can't tell them."

"Yeah, of course. I won't tell them." He paused, looking up at the moths swooping around the street lamp. "And you'll tell me, right? If . . . if you see her?"

Macy's face softened. She even put her hand on his arm. "Of course, I'll tell you."

"I mean my mom."

She sort of laughed—a sharp, quick exhale. "Jesus Christ. I know who you mean. If your mom . . . I'll tell you right away. And I won't let anyone touch her."

They started walking together, heading towards Macy's house. "So," she eventually said, "did Claire tell you about the Halloween party at Trev and Sam's house?"

"Yeah, Sam mentioned something about it."

"Sam, huh?" Macy said, raising her eyebrows like it was a question.

"Yeah. Sam." He didn't know what else to say

about Sam. He didn't really want to talk about Sam with Macy.

They walked in silence for a few more minutes, then Macy said, "So, what are you gonna be?"

Jackson hadn't actually thought much about Halloween. Every fucking day was Halloween as far as he was concerned. "I dunno. Maybe a ghost."

Macy laughed her low, sort-of-laugh again. She sounded tired, but she had a teasing tone to her voice when she said, "And how would you know what one looks like?"

Jackson grabbed her around the waist and tried to swing her up over his shoulder—something he used to do on the playground when they were in middle school. He could usually cover about fifteen feet with her up over his shoulder, legs flailing, before a recess lady would come yell at him that it was "not appropriate playground behavior." This time Macy wriggled out of his arms and started running down the street, shrieking and laughing. She almost sounded hysterical.

"Quiet!" Jackson called out, "One of your neighbors is going to think I'm murdering you."

"Like you could catch me!" she taunted. As if Macy could possibly outrun him. She was, like, two feet tall. But Jackson let her run ahead of him, just out of reach, until they were almost to her house. Then he swung his arms around her waist and held her against his chest so she couldn't twist away again.

She was breathing hard and her face was hot and sweaty when he pressed his mouth to her cheek. "Just don't be an idiot, okay? Promise me?" he said, leaving his cheek against hers while they both caught their breath.

Macy pulled back for a moment, but then rested her head against his chest. Jackson put his chin on the top of her head. Her hood had fallen back while she was running and her hair smelled like the fruity shampoo she always used, but also like the forest. She always smelled nice. "I'm okay," she whispered.

"Just . . . " He tried to think about how to say what he meant. Just stop hiding things from him. Stop taking stupid chances. Stop wandering around in the creepy woods at night. "Just tell me, okay? Next time you want to do something stupid? We can be stupid together."

Chapter Seventeen

Macy didn't hear about the third death until she got to school on Halloween. It was a gorgeous morning—blue sky, the leaves bright and crunchy under her feet as she walked to school. Macy loved the spicy smell of fallen leaves and how she could just barely see her own breath. It made getting up for school on a Monday a little less painful.

Some people were already dressed up for Halloween. Macy saw a baby in a stroller who was dressed like a fly. The man pushing the stroller was a spider and the stroller itself was covered in fake cobwebs—sort of disturbing when she thought about it. She passed Western Winds and smiled at all the pumpkins out front. Macy had tried to keep volunteering at the retirement home, but it was too hard.

First, it was really weird to hear them talk about Lorna—not to mention all the HAVE YOU SEEN ME? posters that were plastered everywhere with her face on them. No one knew what to make of Lorna's disappearance. Did she wander off into the woods somewhere? Did she just get into someone's car? People were always talking about it.

Second, one day Macy had to dispatch a ghost at Western Winds and she thought that Esther saw her do it. The older women had stared past Macy to where the ghost—an old man with a hole from a Tracheotomy in his neck—evaporated into nothing. Macy left that day and didn't return. She kept thinking that she'd go back and say hi to Esther, but she hadn't, and now it had been over a month.

Macy was wearing her Little Red Riding Hood cape over regular clothes. She didn't really like dressing up at school, but the cape was at least something. The bright red of the cape flashed out of the corner of her eye with each step. She figured she'd let Claire help her put together a more complete costume after school.

Dom was waiting for her outside the front of the school. He wasn't dressed like anything, except for a kind of sloppy version of himself. He looked like he hadn't shaved in a while, and his eyes had huge bags under them. "Come on," he said, taking her hand and pulling her around the back of the school. For an instant Macy thought Dom grabbed her hand because, well, he just wanted to hold her hand—like that Beatles' song. The blisters on her hand stung, but she didn't let go. Then she saw Trev and Sam waiting for them on the other side of the building. Their faces looked grim.

She released Dom's hand and crossed her arms. "What?" Macy noticed Jackson was missing and once again her stomach clenched—just like when she was on the phone with her mom when she was at the mall. Ever since Jackson's stupid game with the ghost at the lake, Macy kept thinking about what could have happened—how close it had been.

"Where's Jackson?" she finally asked, just as Dom said, "They found another body."

She felt like cold water was running down her face. Then Jackson came around the corner and she took a deep breath. He walked past Macy and stood next to Sam, who gave him a quick pat on the arm.

"It was another guy," Dom continued, "and his throat was cut, too. This can't be a coincidence."

"Who found him?" Jackson asked.

Dom rubbed his shoulder. He looked at Macy, holding her eyes for a moment, and then looked back to Jackson. "I did."

"Really?" Jackson said in a tone that sounded like he was accusing Dom of something. "Where?"

Dom sighed. "On the beach. I can't sleep sometimes and I go for walks." Macy didn't know that.

She wondered how often he couldn't sleep and if it was the pain that kept him awake. "I found a man down on the beach, a few miles from our house. Really near the school actually."

"You mean near the Door," Macy said. "Is that important?"

"Could be—the Arizona murders were all near the Door. I don't really know if that's part of the ritual or not."

"Wait," Jackson said. "What'd you do? You found this dead body and then what?"

"Shhh," Sam said, kind of smacking Jackson in the arm. "A little louder? Dom came home and told us."

"So you just left him there?" Jackson's lip curled slightly. "You didn't call the police?"

"Of course not," Dom said. "Someone else'll find him. It's not like he's going to be any *more* dead in a few hours."

"Did you see him?" Macy asked. "His ghost, I mean."

"No. I think he was already gone. But his body—" Dom looked a little like he might be sick. "It was just his neck. I didn't see anything else. His neck was . . . "

When he didn't continue, Macy asked, "So, there's only one more, right? For the ritual?" Macy thought about Henry and what he'd said about something waiting behind the Door. Something bad. And he was right there—right by the Door. But Henry couldn't have done it. He couldn't touch anything. It was impossible. She wondered if Henry went anywhere when she wasn't with him. Or did he just wait, watching the light of the Door?

"Yeah. If this is the same ritual, then there's only one left," Dom answered.

Just then a woman from the front office came around the corner. She had a pack of cigarettes in her hand, though there were clear rules against smoking on campus. The woman told them to get to class and then stood there waiting for them to leave, holding the cigarettes behind her back.

As they walked into school, already five minutes late for class, Macy asked "What do we do?"

Macy hadn't directed her question at any one person, but everyone looked to Dom. Before he answered, he took Macy's hand again. This time he just held it, curling his hand around the back of her hand and squeezing her fingers so lightly that it didn't even hurt. "We wait."

After school Macy wanted to go see Henry before it got dark, but she had already made plans with Claire to go over to her house and get ready for the party. Even though Macy had put on a brave face in front of Jackson the night he followed her, it was pretty freaky wandering around with just a flashlight. She needed to ask Henry about the ritual—maybe he knew something about it when he was alive. Maybe he could help them. And part of her—the part that she tried to ignore—wondered if today was finally the day that she should just take care of him. Because what if . . . and that's where she wanted to stop. She didn't want to think about it. What if he was killing people? What if he was never supposed to come back? She thought of Henry and remembered his sad eyes when his hand passed through her arm. He was barely even there. Did it really hurt anything to let him stay?

By the time school got out everyone had heard about the third body. It turned out the dead man was a teacher—a substitute who never showed up for work. His throat had been slashed and he was discovered on the beach in the early morning. But that was all people seemed to know. Macy just hoped that no one had seen Dom leaving the area. What if the police started to ask questions about Dom? Why, for example, did Dom have a gunshot wound? And where were his parents?

What else might the police learn that Macy didn't even know about?

Macy wasn't sure how Dom would answer any of that and it would start to look pretty suspicious. It really annoyed her when Jackson kept insinuating that Dom had something to do with the killings. But Macy thought about how little she actually knew about Dom and the others. Yet she *did* know him. She felt like she could see everything that made up Dom when he looked in her eyes, although he *was* the one who said they should just let the ritual play out and not try to stop the killer.

Macy couldn't just pretend to know for sure what the future might hold. She just had to hope that it wouldn't turn out to be the shittiest option.

Claire's mom picked them up from school, along with Claire's little sister Sabrina, and drove them straight home. After the third body was found, Macy's mom agreed to still let Macy go over to Claire's house as long a parent was driving.

Macy couldn't really blame her mom. She thought about Dom's sister and how his parents didn't know where their daughter was the night she was taken.

Macy felt a little guilty that she'd been lying to her parents so much recently and that she was just going to keep lying. But what choice did she have? Tell them about the ghosts? And Henry? And the Door? And the ritual? Tell them what really happened the night of the Lock-in? Her mom and dad couldn't just fix anything—not the way she used to believe when she was little. They hadn't been able to save Nick and they certainly couldn't do jack shit about Henry or the Door.

Macy told her mom that she and Claire were going over to Jackson's house to pass out candy after getting ready at Claire's house. She knew her mom wouldn't call to check up on them, because she didn't like to bother Jackson's dad.

When they were getting ready in Claire's room,

Claire surprised Macy by pulling a long black dress out of her closet. "This will definitely fit you."

Macy held it to her chest and looked in Claire's full-length mirror. The dress looked like a vampire's lingerie. "First, I'm not wearing this. Second, where did you even get this?"

"I went to a thrift store and bought a few more things since you wouldn't bother to pick out a full costume. What's wrong with it?"

"I don't know . . . how about that this is basically used underwear? And that my boobs would fall out. Wait, you bought a *few* things?"

Claire pulled out something long and white that looked like a wedding dress. "You can freak Dom out!" She hummed the wedding march.

"Uhm . . . no. Next."

Claire went back to the closet. "Okay, final option." She held out another long dress, this time a soft gray color. It had long, flowing sleeves, and a neckline that didn't show most of her chest. It was . . . tasteful. Elegant.

"What's that supposed to be?"

"I dunno. It just looked so pretty." Claire held it up in front of Macy. "Maybe a ghost?"

Macy shook her head and smiled. "So inappropriate," she whispered.

"What?" Claire asked, looking confused.

"Nothing. It's perfect."

Chapter Eighteen

Not many people came to the party, which wasn't that surprising given that most of the school had been permanently grounded after the Lock-in. But the ones who did come brought lots of beer and vodka or rum stolen from their parents. The ratio of booze to student was quite high.

When Macy, Jackson, and Claire arrived, Trev greeted them at the door. He was wearing a Frankenstein costume, complete with those bolts on the sides of his neck. His face was painted a greenish brown, and he had huge fake stitches drawn on his neck in black.

Claire squealed. "You look perfect!" She tugged on his sleeve, making him spin around.

"Claire good," he moaned before laughing. "I can't do that all night. And wasn't Frankenstein's monster supposed to be really smart? In the actual book?"

Macy didn't know that, but she nodded. "Yeah. I think he was really sarcastic, too." Trev grinned with his weirdly blue lips and pulled Claire into the kitchen to get her approval on the food setup. After dodging a few drunk people, Macy saw Sam's red hair from across the room. Jackson immediately left Macy to go talk to her. Sam appeared to be a mermaid, with tight, sparkly blue pants instead of a fin and some kind of really fake-looking sea-shell bra. Was she Ariel? With red hair? Kind of cliché. Macy never did find out what Jackson was—some kind of sailor maybe? He definitely had a nautical thing going on.

Macy had the sudden realization that Jackson's costume was probably supposed to match Sam's (a sailor and a mermaid). She took a long drink from a bottle of champagne someone had left on the coffee table. Macy sneezed and then took another long drink.

After looking everywhere downstairs, Macy finally found Dom in his room. She knocked softly at first, then louder so he could hear her over the thump of the downstairs music. She heard a faint, "Come in," so she pushed open the door.

Dom was sitting at his desk, staring at his computer screen. Two empty beer bottles were lined up neatly on the edge of his desk and he seemed to be working on a third. Macy was pretty sure he wasn't supposed to be drinking with his meds, but she didn't say anything. Dom still wasn't wearing a costume, unless you counted "slightly drunk boy" as a costume.

He smiled as she shut the door behind her. "Macy, you look . . . " He didn't finish that sentence, but took another drink of his beer. She took it out of his hand, drained the last few sips, then set the empty bottle next to the others.

"What're you doing?" she asked, looking at his screen. It was an article that had posted a few hours earlier. Apparently the police had picked up a stranger down by the harbor. He had blood on his clothes.

"Do you think he did it?" Macy asked, peering closer to the picture of the man. He had long hair and a beard, and he wasn't looking straight at the camera, but a little off to the side—like he wasn't looking at her, but at something behind her.

"I don't know. Maybe." Dom stood up. He wasn't that much taller than Macy, but tall enough that she had to tilt her head up to look in his eyes. "You look," he said again, then reached out and touched her cheek. Claire had made Macy's eyes smoky and brushed a light glitter over her face and along her neck. Macy thought she looked pretty damn hot.

"You didn't dress up?" Macy asked him,

stepping even closer. The dress was a little long for her and it brushed along the hardwood floor. Her face was only a few inches from his.

"Sure I did," he laughed, taking a step back. "I'm a Victorian house. The costume's a bit big . . . "

Macy didn't wait another second. She stepped into him—standing on her tiptoes and letting her hands graze his waist. His lips were soft, and when he wrapped his arms around her, she didn't feel nervous or awkward. She felt safe.

"Macy . . . " he murmured, kissing her mouth, then her jaw, and then her lips again.

She smiled against his lips. Claire was right. She should have done this a long time ago.

Macy was still wearing her costume when she went looking for Henry—her red cape wrapped tightly around her. She had told Dom she was just going downstairs to get some food and would be right back. Then she walked out of the house and kept on walking.

It was stupid. She knew it was stupid. She should not be leaving the party to wander around Grey Hills after dark. And why was she leaving Dom? Macy could still feel him on her body. His lips pressed to her collarbone. His hands pulling her dress down over her shoulder so he could kiss her there too. Her hands taking off his shirt, her fingers grazing his wound, pressing her lips just beneath it. His skin was so soft. Perfect.

Why was she leaving? Even now Dom was waiting for her to come back to him. But she had to see Henry.

While she was kissing Dom, Macy couldn't stop the nagging thought in the back of her mind. *Henry.* She needed to go see Henry. It couldn't be him. He couldn't even touch her—how could he have killed anyone? It probably *was* that man, anyway. The guy the police had picked up. He looked crazy. Maybe there wasn't even a ritual at all. Macy knew she should just tell the others about Henry and let them decide what to do. But she knew exactly what they would do. They would kill him. And if he hadn't hurt anyone, then how was that fair? How was any of it fair?

The hem of Macy's dress caught on the blackberry vines as she made her way through the path to the Door. She had walked this way so many times that she knew all of the steps to take—the fallen logs to walk over and the crumbling brick of the old school to step around. She didn't even turn on a flashlight—the glow of the Door was almost enough to see by.

"Henry?" she whispered. He always seemed to come when she called. "Henry?"

"Yes?" He was suddenly right behind her.

She turned, fingering the knife in her pocket.

"You look different," Henry said. His voice was so soft she could barely hear him.

"Oh," Macy put her hand to her face, where

Claire's makeup job was starting to smudge. "It's Halloween. Did you know that?"

"Sure. Like my costume? I came as a ghost." Henry smiled, but it was a grim smile. Macy didn't laugh.

"You look beautiful like that—with your hair down," Henry continued. "I wonder if I would have said that if I was still alive. It's hard to remember sometimes. What I was like then, I mean."

"Do you miss it?"

"Do you miss your dreams?" Henry seemed different, though she couldn't quite place it right away. Then she realized that he didn't look as flickery or see-through. He looked more . . . solid. More real.

"Sometimes," Macy admitted. "Sometimes I know I've just had the best dream, but I can't remember it when I wake up." Several times Macy had dreamed that Nick came back. In the dream it turned out that it was all a big mistake. He wasn't actually dead. He'd just been traveling and had forgotten to tell them where he was going. Nick would walk right through the front door and it all made so much sense. Of course! He had just been on a trip. That explains everything! Every time she woke from those dreams she felt raw and cheated—like someone had been lying to her. Her own brain, she supposed.

"Do you dream now?" Macy didn't want to stop talking. It felt like as long as she was talking to him, it wouldn't end—this little secret world she had created around him.

"I don't think I even sleep." Henry closed the distance between them. "You really are though. Beautiful, I mean. I wish I'd known you when I was alive. You would have liked me. Everyone liked me when I was alive."

"Is that right?" Macy smiled, though she felt a little strange smiling. With the huge moon and her breath floating in front of her face, nothing was quite real. She couldn't see his breath, she realized. Ghosts don't breathe.

Henry flashed her his white, slightly translucent teeth. "I think it was my smile. My mom used to tell me that I had a cat-who-caught-the-canary smile." He reached out and put his hand on her cheek.

She flinched like he had slapped her. "You can't—" she said. Backing away, she pulled out her knife and flipped it open.

He closed the distance again, wrapping his hand in her hair. "I can." He put his other hand on her cheek again, holding her tight. "I think I would have loved you when I was alive. Or maybe you remind me of someone I used to love. But now . . . I don't think it's the same."

"What are you?" Macy asked, transfixed by his hand on her face. She tried to reach out with her mind—to feel the edges of him like she did that first day by the Door. Once again, she felt him push back, only so much stronger. It felt like touching an electric fence.

"I remembered after that first day. I knew exactly what I had to do."

She could see the light of the Door behind his eyes.

"Every day, when you came to see me, I told myself—one more day. Just give her another day. But now there's no more time." He gripped her wrist, pushing her knife hand away from him. She struggled, but he dug his fingers into the tendons of her wrist. Her hand went numb. When he took the knife from her, she felt like she was floating.

"No." Macy tried to shake her head—tried to move away from him, but he held her fast. Her brain filled with a mixture of shock and hysteria that left her feeling one breath away from what was happening to her. What was going to happen. She heard something behind her—a rustling sound, but she couldn't look away from Henry.

"What're you doing?" she whispered, her throat tight. She couldn't get enough air. She needed another breath. One more deep breath. If she could just catch her breath, she could concentrate. Macy didn't need her knife. She was strong—stronger than any of the others. That's what they told her. She pushed harder, feeling her mind beginning to latch onto Henry. She just needed a little more time.

"I'm going to save the world, Macy. And you're going to help me." He leaned forward and pressed his cool lips to her forehead. Then he turned her sharply, so her back was pressed against his stomach. Henry brought his cheek to hers. He was so cold. "Don't worry," he whispered in her ear. "It's not so bad . . . being dead. I promise."

Chapter Nineteen

When Macy left the party, Jackson followed. He didn't even really follow her this time—he just went straight to the Door. Where else was she going to go? He waited for almost ten minutes—she was so slow—and tried to focus his eyes on the Door. Tonight it looked brighter for some reason—more like light reflecting off a window.

When Macy appeared, she looked like she belonged there in the woods. Her cape fluttered in the wind, but it didn't look red in the dark. It looked black.

And when she pulled out her knife, Jackson didn't freeze—not the way he did at the lake, when Sam was first pulled under the water. He didn't hesitate. Jackson couldn't see what she saw, but he ran towards her, his feet ripping through vines and breaking sticks.

Jackson had never had one of those dreams where you are running in slow motion, but that was how it seemed right then. He ran, but it didn't feel like he got any closer. Then Macy turned so she was facing him. Something had her—holding her arm out to the side. The knife was gone from her hand.

As Jackson ran toward her—almost there—he watched a red line grow across Macy's neck. Her eyes went wide and she fell into his arms. "No," he said, pressing his hand to her neck—trying to hold the blood inside her. But it flowed through his fingers. So much blood. Too much. He sank with her to his knees, cradling her in his arms. "It's okay," he whispered into her hair. "You're okay." Macy made a little choking sound and she moved one of her hands up to his—just grazing his fingers with the tips of her gloved hands. He couldn't see her face—just the back of her hair and the curve of her legs as her body went limp against his. Jackson couldn't get his phone out of his pocket—couldn't dial 911—because he had to keep his hand over her throat. The blood was so warm, so sticky. It didn't feel real. None of it could be real.

Macy's blood covered them both and soaked into the ground at the base of the Door. In that moment, the Door grew bright—the light pulsed and rippled, just as Macy had always described it. Jackson blinked tears from his eyes, and then he saw a boy—not Nick—standing beside the Door. He looked familiar, but Jackson didn't think about that. He just thought a single word over and over. *No.*

The boy shook his head and frowned down at Jackson. Then he stepped through the Door and was gone. The Door flickered, wavered. It filled Jackson's eyes, until that was all he could see—that one blinding light. He wanted to close his eyes, because it was like staring into the sun. But he couldn't. And then, when it seemed as though the Door was going to burn out his eyes and devour him from the inside out, he felt something cool brush over his face. It felt like a hand at first, and then like a sharp, stabbing pain on the side of his head. He blinked, and for just an instant he thought he saw a person standing in front of the Door, leaning over him. But then the Door seemed to implode—squeezing into itself until it was just a tiny point of light. Then it winked out completely, the last dying ember from a bonfire extinguishing itself in the wind.